Anna drew a breath.

"But Todd, why move?" she asked him plaintively. "I mean, we're happy here. Aren't we?"

He didn't reply at first. Anna noticed him hesitate for the second time, and the subsequent silence filled the room like an unwelcome blanket of smoke.

"Todd?" Anna turned to look at him, her face suddenly pale and troubled. "Are you trying to tell me you aren't happy?"

He shook his dark head. "Sweetheart— it isn't as simple as that."

SHARON KENDRICK started storytelling at the age of eleven and has never really stopped. She likes to write fast-paced, feel-good romances with heroes who are so sexy they'll make your toes curl!

Born in west London, she now lives in the beautiful city of Winchester—where she can see the cathedral from her window (but only if she stands on tiptoe). She is married to a medical professor—which may explain why the members of her family get more colds than anyone else on the street—and they have two children, Celia and Patrick. Her passions include music, books, cooking and eating—and drifting off into wonderful daydreams while she works out new plots!

You are invited to celebrate two of the most talked about weddings of the decade—lavish marriages where the cream of society gathers in dazzling international settings.

SOCIETY WEDDINGS

Two original short stories in one volume:
Promised to the Sheikh by Sharon Kendrick
The Duke's Secret Wife by Kate Walker
On sale August, Harlequin Presents #2268

Books by Sharon Kendrick

HARLEQUIN PRESENTS®
2239—THE MISTRESS'S CHILD

Don't miss any of our special offers. Write to us at the following address for information on our newest releases.

Harlequin Reader Service
U.S.: 3010 Walden Ave., P.O. Box 1325, Buffalo, NY 14269
Canadian: P.O. Box 609, Fort Erie, Ont. L2A 5X3

Make-Over Marriage

SHARON KENDRICK

THE MILLIONAIRES

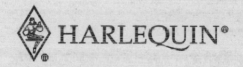

HARLEQUIN®

TORONTO • NEW YORK • LONDON
AMSTERDAM • PARIS • SYDNEY • HAMBURG
STOCKHOLM • ATHENS • TOKYO • MILAN • MADRID
PRAGUE • WARSAW • BUDAPEST • AUCKLAND

To the stunning Kym Westbrook
and her two angelic children, Jody and Bod!

ISBN 0-373-80516-0

MAKE-OVER MARRIAGE

First North American Publication 2002.

This edition published by arrangement with Harlequin Books S.A.

® and TM are trademarks of the publisher. Trademarks indicated with ® are registered in the United States Patent and Trademark Office, the Canadian Trade Marks Office and in other countries.

Visit us at www.eHarlequin.com

Printed in U.S.A.

CHAPTER ONE

TODD TRAVERS removed a ballet shoe from behind the teapot, and said something rather uncomplimentary about it beneath his breath. He briefly contemplated hurling it to the other side of the bright, airy kitchen, but resisted. It would probably disappear for ever in this noisy, chaotic home of his, and he could just imagine the ensuing panic if *that* should happen!

"Don't those girls ever put *anything* away?" he demanded, in a voice so rich and deep and spine-tinglingly sexy that most people meeting him for the first time laboured under the illusion that he was a Shakespearean actor, instead of a businessman with one of the most respected portfolios in London!

Anna lifted her head to look at her husband. She was sitting on the floor, polishing three sets of shoes, and her neck was beginning to ache. Meanwhile, Todd had broken the habit of a lifetime and come home from work unexpectedly early today. And still hadn't told her why!

Her deep blue eyes were dreamy and faraway, but they instantly focused with pleasure on the hard symmetry of her husband's features. Unconsciously, her heart picked up speed as she let her eyes drift adoringly over him, then sighed.

Todd was one of those men who were often described as being too good-looking for their own good—though Anna certainly didn't have any complaints in that department! Tall and fit—with strong, muscular thighs and a lean, hard body—he had all the grace of the natural sportsman. His thick dark hair held the hint of a wave to it, and when he smiled it was like the sun coming out.

In fact, if someone had asked Anna to list any of Todd's less attractive characteristics, she would have been completely stumped, but then she was just a hopeless case where Todd was concerned, still occasionally having to pinch herself in case the whole marriage turned out to be a dream!

Ten years down the line and three children had done nothing to dissipate the sense of wonder she sometimes felt, knowing that she was wedded to a man as downright gorgeous as Todd Travers!

"Mmm?" she questioned absently, carefully putting down the little black shoebrush on the sheet of newspaper. "What was that you said, darling?"

"The girls," he repeated impatiently. "They never seem to put anything away. Do they?"

Anna's eyes swivelled to the French dresser, on which she had placed a large, laughing portrait of their ten-year-old triplets with their butter-coloured curls and their dark blue eyes which were so like their mother's.

It was an extremely flattering photograph, and had been taken by a leading London photographer who had instantly admired the girls' professionalism. But such professionalism was hardly surprising, since Natalia, Natasha and Valentina Travers had been successfully modelling in television commercials for the last two years.

The three girls had been "discovered' by a casting director whose son attended their school in Kensington—the very same school where Anna herself had gone as a child. The triplets had been mad-keen to take part in the proposed supermarket TV campaign, but it had taken a good deal of persuasion before Anna and Todd had been convinced that their daughters' school work would not suffer.

Since then the three girls had worked exclusively for Premium Stores, a vast chain of supermarkets which had outlets all over Britain. They appeared regularly on television advertisements and their smiling faces—so like Anna's—were routinely featured on giant hoardings nationwide. And their schoolfriends were all desperately jealous of them, because, as Valentina had once gleefully put it, "we actually get *paid* to eat chocolate biscuits!"

Seasoned veterans, all three, thought Anna, and her mouth curved into a soft smile as she stared at their mischievous, mobile faces. "I know that they can be a *little* untidy," she told Todd reluctantly, because, quite frankly, if her three daughters had suddenly sprouted wings and sported haloes, it would have come as no surprise to their doting mother!

Her husband's dark brows met in a forbidding ebony line above grey eyes which today looked as wintry as a December sky. "That's hardly surprising," he commented acidly.

Anna's eyes widened in question. "Oh? Why's that?"

"Because you spend your whole life running round after them!" he accused growlingly.

"Todd, I don't—"

"Anna, you *do*," he cut across her. "You know you do! You insist on doing everything for them! Like now, for instance," he accused, sending a dark glower in the direction of the half-polished shoes. "Why do you do so much for them?"

"Because I'm their mother," she answered calmly.

"Other mothers have help," he pointed out.

"Other mothers have careers. I can't justify farming my children out to strangers when I'm not even going out to work, Todd!"

"I don't like to see you cleaning their shoes," he said stubbornly. "That's all."

Anna stopped thinking about whether the girls had matching clean tights for tomorrow's photo-shoot, or whether she should take a lasagne from out of the freezer for supper, or simply start cooking something from scratch—and gave her husband her full attention. The curving shape of his mouth had definitely flattened into an implacable line. She put the lid carefully back on the tin of polish. "Are you angry about something, Todd?"

Their eyes met.

"You don't want to hear about it—"

"Oh, yes, I do," she demurred softly. Her deep blue eyes were curious as she leaned back against her heels to look at him and absent-mindedly lifted her finger to loop a long strand of hair which was tickling her cheek, then tucked it behind her ear.

The small movement hinted at the lush swell of her breasts and Todd felt the slow burn of desire begin to prick heatedly at his skin, even though his wife was doing absolutely nothing to inflame him. Quite the opposite, in fact.

Anna always dressed very practically—a habit she had acquired with three tiny babies to look after, and one which she had never quite lost. She wore a pair of leggings which had already begun to wrinkle at the knee, and a sloppy red cotton sweater which was pretty shapeless. Her buttery blonde hair was scraped back into a ponytail and tied with a velvet ribbon, and she wasn't wearing a scrap of make-up.

And yet...

"Why don't you tell me, Todd?" She scrambled to her feet and looked at him quizzically. "Or shall I fetch you a drink first?"

He shook his head, then looked into her trusting face and almost changed his mind, aware of the bombshell he was about to drop into her lap. "I don't want a drink," he told her emphatically. "Let's go next door and sit down, shall we?"

Anna nodded and followed him into the sitting room, whereupon he immediately flopped his angular frame onto one of the large, squashy green sofas, and sighed.

Anna slid onto the far end of the sofa and smiled at him encouragingly, thinking that her normally equable husband was in a very irritable mood today. Though, come to think of it, hadn't he been oddly distracted for the past few weeks now? And every time she had asked him if something was wrong he had just shaken his dark head rather impatiently.

Anna was beginning to lose patience herself; she was much too busy for all these guessing games. If something was wrong, he should jolly well tell her! "So tell me what's troubling you, Todd."

He hesitated, choosing his words carefully because he had an extremely strong suspicion that his wife was going to object to what he was about to say. And object very strongly, too. "Sweetheart—"

"Oh, for goodness' sake, Todd—spit it out!"

He smiled briefly, because she was the only woman in the world he would allow to get away with speaking to him like that! "Perhaps it's time that we thought about moving..."

It was the last thing Anna had expected to hear. If Todd had suddenly announced that he wanted the five of them to go back-packing across the Arizona desert, she could not have been more surprised. *"Moving?"* She sat bolt upright on the sofa and stared at him in dismay.

They had started their married life in this mansion flat, brought up three lively triplets within its spacious walls, and stayed together there as a family, despite all the odds and the dire predictions of the few people who had known them at the very beginning. "Moving?" said Anna again, only more faintly this time.

Todd nodded. "That's right. It isn't *such* a bizarre suggestion, is it, sweetheart? Lots of people do it all the time! Think about it sensibly."

But Anna had discovered that thinking sensibly was easier said than done, especially since she had become a mother. Because in the ten years since she had given birth to the triplets her brain had gone completely to mush. From someone who at school could add up a whole line of figures in her head, she was sometimes reduced to counting on her fingers when the triplets had friends over to tea and she needed to calculate how many jam sandwiches they would need!

She put it down to motherhood, and having to remember at least twenty things at the same time, but whatever the cause she was no longer terribly good at thinking through a problem logically. She tended to fire off at the deep end if she felt rattled—and rattled was exactly what she felt right now.

That, and insecure.

This flat was her nest and her haven; she had lived here for as long as she could remember—long before she'd married Todd. And they were happy here. The last thing in the world she wanted was to uproot them all. "But I don't want to move *anywhere*, Todd," she told her husband firmly.

A muscle moved dangerously by the side of his mouth. "No, I realise that. But you can't just dismiss the suggestion like that, Anna!"

No. He was right. She couldn't. Not if she wanted to win him round to her way of thinking. Because Todd Travers was one of those infuriatingly cool and reasonable men who always had an answer for everything. And if Anna burst into noisy and hysterical tears—which was what she *felt* like doing at that precise moment—and made a passionate announcement stating that she couldn't bear to leave, then Todd would simply demolish all her arguments by the sneaky use of logic.

Anna drew a deep breath. "But Todd, why move?" she asked him plaintively. "I mean, we're happy here. Aren't we?"

He didn't reply at first. Anna noticed him hesitate

for the second time, and the subsequent silence filled the room like an unwelcome blanket of smoke.

"Todd?" Anna turned to look at him, her face suddenly pale and troubled. "Are you trying to tell me you *aren't* happy?"

He shook his dark head. "Sweetheart—it isn't quite as simple as that."

Anna stilled as she heard the sombre note in his voice and immediately leapt to one very gloomy conclusion as to what her husband might *really* be trying to tell her. "Are you t-trying to tell me that you're seeing someone else?" she demanded shakily, because her stomach was tied up in tight little knots as she asked the question.

Todd actually burst out laughing. "Oh, Anna—"

"Don't you 'Anna' me!" she stormed back, but her relief at his reaction was so immense that she found herself picking up a cushion and hurling it at him. He caught it as easily as blinking. "If there's another woman in your life, then I darned well want to know about it, Todd Travers!"

Todd put the cushion down and stood up, and Anna was horrified to find herself gazing lustfully at his thighs. How was it possible to be *this* angry with a man, she wondered, and yet to know that if that same man wandered over and started making love to her she would be hard-pushed to resist him? Not that he would, of course. Not right now, on the sofa, in broad daylight. Todd was a man who had always kept his formidable sexual appetites strictly under control...having three children born at the same time had made sure of that!

"There *is* no other woman," he told her softly. "As

well you know. I am simply not interested in other women—''

''Aren't you?'' she queried, only slightly mollified and unwilling to let the subject drop.

''Even if I had the time or the energy—*ouch*!'' he exclaimed as a second cushion this time found its target. ''You are a very good shot, Mrs Travers!'' he mused, rubbing at his shadowed chin where the embroidered cushion had hit him. ''Perhaps you should take up golf?''

''Please don't try and change the subject, Todd!'' she warned him sweetly. ''And if it's not another woman, then you'd better start explaining why you're not happy!''

''Now you *are* putting words in my mouth,'' he accused quietly. ''I didn't actually say that, did I?''

He moved to stand directly in front of her then, the loose cut of his Italian trousers not quite concealing the powerful shafts of his thighs, and Anna felt consumed with longing.

''Can I sit down?'' he questioned, indicating the space beside her.

''Since when did you start asking?'' she asked breathlessly.

''Since you started hurling soft furnishings at me, and then decided to glower at me as if I were the most heinous villain in history,'' he responded silkily. ''So can I?''

''Suit yourself,'' she shrugged, aware that she was not responding in a very adult way, but quite at a loss to know how to stop it, since she suspected from the grim expression on his face that Todd was about to tell her something she most definitely didn't want to hear.

She noted that he positioned his long-legged frame at some distance from her, and was grateful for the physical space between them, at least. Because she was suddenly and quite overwhelmingly aware of him. And her hands were shaking...

"You asked if we were happy here," he began, but he was frowning.

"And you gave me an evasive answer."

"Well, try this for straightforwardness." He ran his fingers through the thick, already ruffled waves of his dark hair and stared at her. "Of course I've been happy here."

She noted his use of the past tense. "Well, then?"

"I'm happy now," he amended softly. "I just think we could be even happier."

"And just what is that supposed to mean?"

Todd sighed, wishing that he *had* opted for that drink, after all. He had been dreading this moment for too long now, but he could put it off no longer. "Just that we have been very, very blessed—I'm aware of that, Anna. We live in a large and very comfortable apartment—"

"Which is situated right slap bang in the middle of the capital!" she prompted immediately.

"As you say."

"We couldn't get more central if we tried, Todd! Could we?"

"No, indeed. But we also have three rapidly growing daughters," he reminded her drily. "Who very soon may no longer be contented with sharing a bedroom, no matter how vast that bedroom might be," he added as he saw his wife open her mouth and correctly anticipated her objection to that particular statement.

"The triplets could never *bear* to be separated!" objected Anna as she recalled the many battles she had had over the years. Why, even on holidays they wouldn't contemplate the idea of different rooms. "They've always said that!"

"Have you asked them recently?"

Something in his tone alerted Anna to discussions from which she had clearly been excluded. "No," she answered steadily. "But I presume from your voice that you have?"

"I *have* been talking to the girls about lifestyles in general," he told her unwillingly, wondering why he should feel as though he had committed some kind of crime.

"But you clearly decided that I shouldn't be privy to this particular discussion?" she queried tartly. "Or was there more than one?"

Todd drummed his long fingers so that they sounded like galloping hooves on the arm of the velvet sofa. "Don't make it sound like a felony I've committed against you, Anna," he warned her softly. "You have lots of conversations with the girls which do not include me."

Anna bit back the temptation to tell him that talks about whether they needed new clothes, or nagging at them to do their homework, were hardly in the same league as moving house!

She looked directly into stormy grey eyes, narrowed now so that only a gleam of silver was visible, their expression shaded by the lush fringing of his dark lashes. "So what exactly did you all discuss?" she asked him. "And how did the subject come up?"

He decided to come clean. "It was on your birthday—when I was looking after them. Remember?"

She most certainly did! For her twenty-eighth birthday Todd had bought her a ticket for a day's pampering at one of London's most luxurious female-only health clubs.

Privately, Anna had thought the gift slightly wasted on someone as uninterested in her appearance as *she* was. She had spent the day being pummelled and pounded, sweating in a sauna and then being forced to plunge into an icy tub. She had had her skin massaged with unctuous creams and her nails buffed and manicured, then, after a lunch which consisted entirely of some inedible form of plant life, she had arrived home refreshed and rejuvenated, but with the most enormous appetite!

"So the subject just happened to come up, did it?" enquired Anna suspiciously. "Just like that? The girls suddenly turned to you and said, 'Daddy—we want to move!'"

He didn't respond. Just sat there with a studiedly patient expression as he returned her accusing stare.

"Well?" prompted Anna sarcastically, infuriated by the maddeningly *reasonable* look on his face! How *dare* he be so reasonable? "Was that what happened?"

"Are you going to give me a chance to tell you?" he enquired coolly. "Or are you going to continue speaking for me so melodramatically?"

"I think I need a drink," said Anna suddenly, and couldn't miss Todd's look of surprise at her request.

She, who normally took alcohol on high days and holidays only, and then in such tiny amounts that any more than a glass of wine could render her very tipsy indeed!

"I'll fetch us one," said Todd instantly, and escaped into the kitchen where he busied himself with opening wine and getting glasses out of the cupboard while he decided how best to continue a discussion which was not going at all the way he had intended.

Anna noticed that he had chosen a very expensive bottle indeed and raised her eyebrows as he carried the tray into the sitting room. "It must be *very* bad news," she joked darkly as he handed her a glass of wine.

Todd ignored that as he sat back down beside her and sipped at his drink, then put his glass firmly down on the table and turned to her. "It's just that I don't spend as much time with the girls as I'd always like, so on your birthday I told them that they could do exactly what they wanted to do—within reason, of course—as a special treat."

"That was very sweet of you," said Anna automatically as she tried her wine.

"That's when Tally told me, in the gloomiest voice imaginable, that it would be impossible for her to do what she really wanted to do, because she simply wasn't allowed."

"This is all to do with horses, I suppose?" said Anna slowly as she thought of Natalia, first-born of their triplets, who was completely and utterly pony-mad. She spent all her allowance on pony and horse magazines and every book she read for pleasure had an equestrian theme.

"Yes, it is," Todd agreed, rather grimly. "She asked me rather plaintively why she wasn't allowed to have a horse of her own."

"Because she knows as well as I do that horse-riding is far too risky," sighed Anna. "All three of them are aware that they cannot take part in any kind of dangerous sport—why, it's even written into their contract! The casting director told her right at the beginning that if she breaks an arm or a leg, then it could spell disaster for the campaign."

"Which would be the end of the world, no doubt?" questioned Todd slowly. "Disaster for the campaign?"

The mocking tone in his voice made Anna's head jerk up swiftly, and something indefinable she read in his eyes made her put her barely touched glass of claret quickly back onto the table.

"And just what is *that* supposed to mean?" she asked him in a low voice.

Todd's gaze was very steady. "It doesn't *mean* anything, Anna," he responded softly. "I was just wondering if it would be so terrible if the girls stopped working for Premium Stores—"

"Of course it would!" returned Anna immediately. "You know how lucky they are to have that contract! Other children—more experienced by far than ours—would have absolutely *leapt* at the chance!"

"You sound like a real showbiz mum," Todd told her critically, and Anna went cold with both indignation and fear because Todd never usually used that horrible, disapproving tone with her.

"That isn't fair and you know it!" she retorted. "I never went looking for fame for the girls—fame found *them*! We discussed it carefully with all three of them before we let them go ahead with the advertisements— you know we did! And we both agreed that so long as it didn't interfere with their school work they could carry on doing it. And it *doesn't* interfere with their school work, does it?''

''Not so far,'' answered Todd cautiously. ''But—''

''And they earn heaps of money for what they do,'' insisted Anna quickly.

''But we're hardly on the breadline, are we, sweetheart?'' he commented drily as he let his gaze drift around the elegantly proportioned room, taking in the high ceiling and the costly chandelier which glittered like a million rainbow icicles.

''Okay,'' she conceded, with a shrug of her shoulders. ''They aren't doing it for the money! They're doing it because they absolutely love it!''

Todd frowned. ''They used to. I think they love it less than when they first started,'' he pointed out.

''Do they really? That's something *else* they've told you, but omitted to mention to me, is it?'' Anna knew that her voice sounded waspish and peeved, but she seemed unable to do anything about it.

She felt hurt.

Badly hurt.

She had given birth to the triplets when she was still seventeen—why, she had been little more than a child herself—and had always considered her relationship with her girls to be incredibly close. So it was something of a shock to discover that they had been grumbling to their father and completely excluding her!

Todd observed his wife's white, angry face and wondered just why this discussion was going so disastrously wrong. The last thing he wanted was to antagonise Anna. He thought about how smoothly topics could be raised and discussed in the workplace and wondered why discussions at home always seemed to get fraught with emotion and lack of logic.

He decided to try again. "On that day you were away at the health club, the girls and I sat down and had quite a long chat," he admitted.

"So it would seem," came her stony response. "And what *exactly* did you sit down and chat about?"

Todd took another mouthful of wine as he thought about how best to word his daughters' complaints about a lifestyle which most of their peers envied. "They *have* loved working for Premium Stores," he told Anna with a placatory smile which chilled her. "As they themselves said—how many children get plucked from obscurity to star in a supermarket advertising campaign which fits in so well with the rest of their lives?"

"Exactly!" responded Anna triumphantly. "Plus they've got to meet all kinds of celebrities, done the sorts of things that most children only dream of..." Her voice tailed off rather wistfully as she recalled the memorable occasion when Tally, Tasha and Tina had served a world-famous rock star with fizzy cola on stage, to launch Premium Stores' new range of diet drinks. Why, the excitement at school had taken *weeks* to die down!

"Nobody is denying that the job has given them opportunities that they would never normally have had," Todd said soothingly. "But they've been working for two years now."

"And Premium want them to carry on working for them," said Anna stubbornly. "Indefinitely."

Todd decided that the time had come to stop pussy-footing around. And if his wife was refusing to listen, then he was going to have to *make* her! "Yes, I know that the company still want them, Anna. But the point you seem to be missing is that although the contract is both lucrative and exciting it is also very restrictive."

"It's an exclusive contract," defended Anna. "That's why."

Todd shook his head. "I am not talking about the restrictive clause which prevents the girls from working for anyone else while they are contracted to Premium," he argued. "But restrictive in a much wider sense. Tasha is doing particularly well at school—"

"I know!" Anna beamed proudly. "And they want her to sit for a scholarship to her next school!"

"But if she sits for a scholarship she'll need to study, won't she?" said Todd. "And when will she find the time to do that, with all the demands that Premium make on her time?"

"She could try watching less television, for a start," said Anna, echoing the words of mothers the world over, but Todd shook his dark head vigorously.

"That isn't fair, and you know it. She doesn't watch much television, and she's entitled to watch *some*, surely? If she can't have any bona fide relaxation time because of school and study and filming, then that isn't much of a life for a ten-year-old, now, is it?

"Meanwhile, Tally is prevented from riding a horse because of the injuries she might sustain," he continued inexorably. "And, what is more, she has saved up enough money for a horse of her own so it's doubly disappointing for her never to be able to ride."

"But we live in Knightsbridge!" retorted Anna spikily. "How on earth could she possibly have a horse of her own when we haven't any room for one? Where are you proposing we stable it? Outside Harrods?"

"Exactly!" breathed Todd, and Anna got the distinct feeling that she had fallen straight into a trap of his making. "Knightsbridge is not the kind of place where people keep pets! We don't have room for a horse, or a dog," he went on, his words coming so automatically that it sounded as though he had been thinking about the subject for ages.

Had he? wondered Anna fleetingly. And, if so, then why the hell hadn't he talked it over with her before? Why was he just springing it on her now, like this?

"We also don't have apple trees which are covered in fragrant blossom in springtime and heavy with succulent fruit in the autumn," he said, his voice growing more impassioned than she had heard it for a long time.

"There are no streams for the girls to paddle in before they grow too old and disdainful to do so," he continued, his grey eyes dark and smoky. "No wild flowers for them to gather to make garlands for their hair. They won't see rabbits scampering playfully across fields or hear owls hooting at night."

"You've been reading too many books about the country!" joked Anna with the nervous smile of the born city-dweller, but there was no answering smile on the chiselled lips of her husband. "You forgot to mention the mud and the midges and being cut off whenever the weather turns bad!''

''You forget that I grew up in the country, Anna,'' he contradicted her softly. ''And, while my memories may be *vaguely* rose-tinted, I can assure you that I am only too aware of all the drawbacks of living out in the sticks.''

Anna remembered how this whole conversation had started—with moving. She had thought that was bad enough, but now it sounded as though Todd wanted a whole radical lifestyle change. Well, they were a partnership. He couldn't force her and the girls to go and live in the country if they didn't want to, and she *definitely* didn't want to!

But how to convince Todd of that?

She stretched her arms above her head as she played for time and, noticing a tiny muscle flicker in Todd's cheek, a daring idea came to her as she thought of a way which might shelve this whole awkward discussion.

Anna was panicking. She had spent most of her life in this very flat. Her father had sold the freehold to Todd very cheaply as a wedding present because Todd, being Todd, had refused to accept the place as a gift. She couldn't *imagine* living anywhere else. Didn't *want* to imagine living anywhere else!

She thought about how frantic their lives were these days. Perhaps she hadn't been paying her husband enough attention recently? That was what all the women's magazines always warned you about, wasn't it? Wives who took their husbands for granted. Was that why he looked so moody and out-of-sorts this evening?

And yet she had one very effective weapon in her armoury which might bring Todd round to her way of thinking—if only she had the courage to use it...

"Phew!" She sighed huskily and wiped the back of her hand across her bone-dry forehead. And suddenly her plan no longer seemed so bizarre because something in the alert and watchful poise of *his* body had started her aching for him... Anna cleared her throat and her voice came out in a sultry little whisper of its own accord. "It's become terribly h-hot in here, hasn't it?"

Todd knew from the sudden tremble in her voice what his wife wanted and he felt his own body stir in response, partly because he desired her very much, and partly because it was not what they would normally have done.

They hardly *ever* went to bed in the middle of the afternoon; he was usually working and when he wasn't, well—there simply weren't the opportunities with three lively and curious children around. And Anna was usually so sweetly shy about sex. She must want to stay in London very much indeed, if she was prepared to seduce him in broad daylight!

He ignored the question in his mind about whether making love right now was going to be enough to paper over all the cracks which had been revealed in their relationship today. Because right now he didn't particularly care. Anna had deliberately lit the touchpaper; let Anna take the consequences.

"You're hot, are you?" he enquired deliberately.

"Mmm. *Boiling*." In an unhurried manner which belied her trembling fingers, Anna peeled off her baggy sweater to reveal a tee-shirt underneath. It wasn't a particularly new or a particularly clinging tee-shirt, yet it moulded the heavy lushness of her breasts to perfection and Anna grew aware that Todd was watching her movements obsessively. "There," she told him huskily, in a voice which sounded awfully decadent to her own ears.

The muscle in his cheek flickered convulsively now, and Todd knew that he was caught in the silken bonds of sexual desire. "Then why don't you take something else off?" he suggested in a murmur, wondering why a corny request which would have made him flinch if he had heard himself making it in, say, the office should sound so good and so right and so *appropriate* right now.

"Wh-why don't you?" she countered shakily, her nerve deserting her.

He needed no second bidding. He leaned forward, his eyes smoky, his mouth a curve of hungry antici-pation as he let it drift over her open lips in a lingering kiss. Then he let his hand stray beneath her tee-shirt to cup her breast possessively in his palm.

Anna closed her eyes and gave a greedy moan of pleasure, because the unexpectedness of her urge to seduce him, and Todd's gratifyingly eager response to it, was turning her on very much.

"Where are the triplets?" he wanted to know.

"E-extra-curricular activities," gasped Anna as she struggled to string her words together coherently. "Saskia is bringing them home."

"And what time are they back?" he demanded, his thumb now tantalising her nipple beneath the crisp lace of her brassière so that he felt it harden and thrust against his flesh.

"We've g-got just under an hour," shuddered Anna breathily, trying to remember the last time they had made love like this. Years, she realised, with a sinking feeling. It had been years and years.

She pulled uselessly at his fine silk shirt, and frantically tried to unbuckle his belt, but as he shook her hands off he noticed that his own were trembling like a schoolboy's. He wanted her so much he could hardly think straight and he couldn't remember feeling quite this hot in a long, long time...

Had their bitter words added fuel to his desire? he wondered. Was that what happened after ten years of marriage—that you needed harsh words to turn you on so much you couldn't think straight?

"Oh, Todd!" gasped Anna, every pore on fire with wanting as her fingers slid sinuously over the hard muscle of his torso. "Please!"

But old habits died hard and Todd shook his head, even though it took every bit of self-control he possessed.

They had spent almost all of their ten years together with children around the place, and they had never made love with an audience, not even when the girls were tiny babies. Neither of them had thought that it seemed quite *right* to lose themselves in sensual pleasure when there were one or more infants snuffling away in the same room. As Todd had often remarked—children didn't exactly enhance the *mood* for making love! While Anna had wondered whether that was because children were often the unexpected consequences of making love.

Like theirs...

"Not here," he growled, his heart pounding hotly

in his chest as he forced himself to resist the appeal in her big blue eyes. "What if the girls come back early?"

"Then—"

"Shh," he urged as he stood up and bent to lift her off the sofa. Unhampered by her weight, he began to carry her towards the bedroom, half-resenting the fierce need she had aroused in him which had made all thoughts of moving fly straight out of the window.

But reason was only temporarily obscured by desire, and Todd resolved to continue the discussion with his wife once he had slaked that desire.

While Anna, who was almost feverish at the prospect of making love with her husband in the middle of the afternoon, clung to him tightly as he set her down on the bed and began to peel off her leggings, mistakenly and rather complacently believing that the subject of moving was now closed...

CHAPTER TWO

IN THE soft light of the late-afternoon sun Anna's heartbeat began to lessen, and she smiled to herself as she ran one lazy finger over Todd's sweat-slicked hip.

"Mmm," he murmured in response, catching her hand and guiding it to an infinitely more intimate part of his anatomy, and Anna sucked in a breath of shocked and delighted pleasure as she felt her husband harden beneath her fingers.

"Todd!" she gasped, but boldly left her hand where it was to make tiny stroking movements.

"Anna!" he mocked on a groan of pleasure, and levered himself up to lean on his elbow, looking down at her rose-flushed face and the silky blonde hair which lay in tousled strands all over the pillow. He picked up one buttery gold lock and twisted it between his fingers, his expression distracted, knowing that if she continued doing what she was doing...

Gritting his teeth with effort, Todd pushed Anna's hand away.

"*Oh!*" she pouted.

"Not now, sweetheart," he said brusquely, even though his body was screaming out for more of the magic she was weaving with her feather-light touch. "How long do we have undisturbed?"

Anna's eyes flicked to the clock which stood on her

bedside table. "Just over half an hour," she yawned.
Her eyes were rueful as she thought back to their fren-
zied lovemaking. "It all happened terribly quickly,
didn't it?"

"Mmm." He smiled with memory. "But you still
enjoyed it?"

Anna blushed, a habit she had never quite lost,
much to her chagrin and her husband's immense pleasure. "You know I did," she responded in a low
voice, but her thoughts were a mass of confusion. It
had been wonderful, yes, but it had been lovemaking
on a different scale to the one she was used to. It had
been frantic even before they'd got into the bedroom,
with Todd pulling the clothes away from her body in
an almost out-of-control way which was nothing like
his usual teasing finesse.

Anna sat up in the rumpled bed and blonde hair
streamed down over her naked breasts. "I'd better get
up—"

He laid a hand on her arm. "Not yet, you're not."

She turned to him wearing a smile of delight which
was mixed with slight exasperation. "But darling, you
just said there wasn't time..."

But he shook his head. "Not to make love again,
Anna," he said seriously. "That wasn't what I meant.
I want to talk."

"Talk?" The acrid taste of fear formed itself into a
cold lump in Anna's throat and, in order to distract
herself from the determined expression glinting in the
depths of her husband's grey eyes, she jumped out of
bed and hunted around for her knickers. "Talk about
what, Todd?" she questioned brightly.

"What we were talking about before you started

pouting and flaunting that luscious body at me. About moving,'' came his stern response as he watched her slide her sensible navy blue panties over her pale thighs and briefly wondered why she never wore the outrageous scraps of nonsense he brought back for her whenever he went abroad.

"But I thought we'd said everything there was to say on the subject,'' she objected, hooking the clasp of her bra behind her back.

Todd shook his head. "Oh, no, sweetheart,'' came his emphatic reply. "I think that *you* said everything you had to say on the subject—namely, that you didn't want to move.''

"Oh!'' Her mouth trembled as she listened to Todd riding roughshod over her objections. "So my opinion counts for nothing, does it?''

Todd sighed. "Of course it does! In fact, if it hadn't been for the fact that you so patently wanted to stay put, I would have brought up the subject of moving out to the country years ago!''

"And I would have had the same objections then as I do now!'' she retorted.

Trying a different tack, he put his hands behind his head, and, leaning back against the pillows, gave her a slow smile. "What exactly do you do in the city that you won't be able to do in the country?''

Anna looked at him assessingly. So he was treating her to the logical approach, was he? She wondered if he realised just how patronising he sounded. "Go to the theatre,'' she said immediately. "And to concerts. Then there are the art galleries and the parks—oh, and all the specialist shops.''

"And if we lived close enough to another city? How

would that be? So that you could still do all those things.''

''But why would we want to? We're settled *here*, Todd,'' she prevaricated. ''You know we are.''

''Yes,'' he conceded. ''But we can just as easily settle somewhere else.'' He saw her mutinous expression, and decided that it might be prudent to backtrack. ''Oh, I'm not being naive, sweetheart. I know it won't be easy to just pack up our things and—''

''Then why *do* it?'' Anna demanded, angry that Todd seemed contented to turn their world upside down on what sounded like little more than a whim.

''For all the reasons we discussed earlier—more space around the place, and a better quality of life for the triplets—''

''But not for me?''

''For all of us,'' he corrected her gently. ''You know that in your heart, sweetheart.''

Any minute now and she would burst into tears.

Anna pulled her crumpled tee-shirt violently down over her head, emerging with her blonde hair flattened like golden skin against her scalp. She shook it free. ''And what's brought this on all of a sudden?'' she asked him. ''Is it just Tally complaining that she can't have a horse?''

He shook his head. ''Not at all. That was coincidental.''

''What, then?''

He shrugged his broad shoulders. ''Because I needed to take a long-term view of my affairs, and I realised that there was absolutely no need for me to be based in London any more. Communication systems today mean that I can work from almost anywhere. Plus you know how long it takes me to get to work.''

Anna nodded. He did have a point. The traffic was so heavy in the mornings that Todd had taken to leaving for the office at the crack of dawn, and often he didn't arrive home until she was putting the triplets to bed. Sometimes even later. No wonder he was always so tired.

And it was no earthly good telling him to cut back on his hours, either, even though he had earned enough to keep them all for several lifetimes. Because the work ethic was deeply ingrained in Todd's nature, the habit of a lifetime hard to break. Todd worked hard because he was a driven man, and like so many driven men he *needed* to work hard. Circumstances in his youth had seen to that.

''Surely we could come to some sort of compromise?'' she suggested, before adding rather irritably, ''And for goodness' sake can't you get up and put some clothes on, Todd? The girls will be back any minute now.''

He grinned as he slid off the side of the bed and pulled on a pair of jeans, and Anna found that she couldn't tear her eyes away from him. He was like a sumptuous feast she couldn't get enough of, and her fingers were just itching to caress the broad, tanned satin of his bare skin once again.

He looked up from buttoning up his shirt and gave her a tender smile. ''You want us to climb straight back into that bed over there, don't you, Anna Travers?''

Anna coloured. ''No, I don't.''

He came over to stand in front of her, and gently

lifted her chin with his finger. "Don't be shy, sweet-heart. You certainly weren't being shy a little while back! I wondered what had got into you, until I realised that *I* had!"

"Todd!" Anna bit her lip as she remembered how ruthlessly he had dealt with her clothes, stripping them from her body like a man on fire.

"There's nothing wrong with admitting that we still want and need each other, you know," he continued softly. "I hope that our mutual desire might even escalate as the years go by! And that's another reason for wanting to move. We may have space here, but we don't have many rooms. And rooms equal privacy."

"Don't we have enough privacy?"

He shook his head emphatically. "Heck, Anna," he continued, with the fluency of someone who had thought an argument right through. "The girls are right next door to us as it is—so what do you suppose is going to happen as they become teenagers and realise why Mummy is moaning such a lot?"

"Todd!" She blushed hotly.

"Quite apart from having to keep quiet—" he frowned "—I should think our chances of making spontaneous love will continue to be infinitesimally small—that is, unless we decide to do something positive about it!

Anna finished pulling on her leggings and turned on him. "And what's got into *you* all of a sudden, Todd Travers?" she demanded. "Do you suppose that other men would attempt to uproot their wives and families just so that they could get *more sex*?"

He had been as tolerant and as understanding as he

knew how, but now Todd went pale with anger at her insult. "So you think that's what this is all about?" he asked, in a voice which was dangerously quiet. "Sex?"

"I don't know," she answered wearily. "You tell me. What else could it be? A mid-life crisis? In which case, at thirty-three aren't you a little young to be experiencing that?"

"Damned right I am!" he agreed heatedly. "But maybe you're right. Maybe it *is* some kind of crisis, only you just haven't had the time or the inclination to notice it before—"

"Todd—" she cut in, as shocked at the brutal look of anger on his face as by the fact that they seemed to be having a pretty significant row. "You don't mean that!"

"Don't I?" he demanded, as fiercely as she'd ever heard him speak. "How do you know *what* I mean? You never listen if it doesn't happen to correspond with what *you* want, do you? And it's about time you heard me out, Anna Travers!"

"Go on, then," she responded, in a shocked, low voice.

He drew in a great breath of air. "Don't you ever feel that we're in some kind of rut?"

"A rut?" she echoed in disbelief.

"Sure." He saw the bewildered look on her face and his mouth softened as he put a hand out to touch her, but she pushed him away.

"I thought you wanted to talk," she said coldly.

He nodded. She was right. Sex had already distracted them from the subject once. "Anna, you grew up in this flat," he sighed. "We've spent all our married life here. We brought up our three babies here and now we're running out of space. I think we've outgrown it.''

His words had a chilling finality about them, as though that area of their life was now over, and Anna felt a shiver of apprehension ice its way down the entire length of her spine. She swallowed down the fear which had risen thickly in her throat like bile.

''I hear what you're saying, Todd,'' she told him quietly.

''Well, that's good,'' came his cautious reply.

Tears threatened to spring up behind her eyes. ''And you're admitting to me for the first time ever what we've both always known—that I trapped you into marriage by getting pregnant! If you'd never met me, you would never have found yourself in this supposedly *terrible* situation—and you could have gone ahead and married your beloved Elisabeta!''

His grey eyes narrowed into splinters of slate. ''Please don't say things in the heat of the moment that you might later regret, Anna!''

But she noticed he didn't deny her words. ''In that case, I'd better not say anything else at all,'' she told him flatly.

He opened his mouth to reply, but the loud ringing on the front doorbell heralded the arrival of the triplets and he decided to let the subject drop. For the moment.

As Anna prepared to walk past her husband he made a conciliatory attempt to catch her in his arms, but she stood clear of his embrace, still wounded by the implications of what he had said to her.

''Just think about everything I've said, Anna,'' he urged her as the ringing increased in volume and in frequency. "That's all I ask. Just consider it. Will you do that for me?"

Put that way, how could she refuse?

Anna risked a quick glance in the mirror as she followed Todd out of the bedroom. She looked absolutely frightful! Her hair was mussed and her cheeks were a giveaway red, and she became acutely aware that she had put her navy blue knickers on back to front! Still, none of the girls was about to notice *that*! She grabbed an elastic band, then scraped her hair back in its habitual ponytail.

Todd opened the front door and there was a whirl of green uniforms and flying blonde curls as three young girls entered the flat like dervishes and began speaking excitedly at the same time, as they had been doing ever since they'd first learned to talk.

"Mummy, Hannah Phipps who writes those horse books is *visiting our school* after Christmas, and I'm to present her with a bouquet of flowers!"

"Mummy, they've given me the part of the wicked witch in the summer play and I'm supposed to give you a list of what I need for costumes—but I've lost it!"

"Mummy, I sat an extra Latin paper, just for fun, only I got the whole thing right, and Mrs McFadden is *seriously* pleased with me!"

"That's sad!"

"It is *not* sad—Mrs McFadden says I'll probably get a Headmaster's Accommodation!"

"Sadder still!"

Anna's mouth softened into a wide smile of loving pride as she surveyed her triplet daughters—identical to look at, but so very different in character. They had inherited their pale, freckle-dusted skin, their cobalt eyes and golden hair directly from her, but whereas her hair was straight, theirs was a mass of uncontrollable curls. They were tall for their age, and their rangy, athletic build came straight from Todd. "Hello, darlings!" she beamed as she hugged each one fiercely in turn. "What clever girls you all are!"

Natalia, Natasha and Valentina were known affectionately as Tally, Tasha and Tina. Tally and Tasha had been born late on February 13th, but their sister hadn't joined them until two minutes after midnight on St Valentine's day. So she never did get christened Nerissa, which had been her parents' original intention, but everyone who knew her decided that "Tina' suited her loving and slightly scatty personality far better than Nerissa would have done!

"Daddy, why are you home from work so early?" asked Tasha curiously, her intelligent eyes flicking from her mother to her father with interest.

"I...sort of...took the afternoon off," explained Todd lamely, and Anna had to try very hard not to smile, their angry spat temporarily forgotten. Rarely, if ever, had she seen her husband look quite so much at a loss for words!

"Oh. I see. And why is your shirt on inside out?" Tasha added innocently.

"Er...juice and biscuits for three hardworking and worn out girls, is it?" enquired Todd hurriedly.

"Oh, yes, *please*, Daddy!" trilled the three in unison.

"And for you, darling?" Todd looked directly at Anna.

Their eyes met over three silky blonde heads and

the unmissable look of determination in her husband's grey eyes made Anna dread the resumption of their talk.

"Tea, please," she told him calmly, grateful for a bit of breathing space.

There was a lull while Todd clattered around in the kitchen and Anna brushed the triplets' wayward hair and exclaimed over offerings brought home from their art class.

And, although she tried very hard not to think about it, her words came back to haunt her as she realised that for the first time ever she had had the courage to speak the truth during her row with Todd.

She had never meant to, but facts were facts, and, yes, she *had* trapped Todd Travers into a marriage he had never intended...

CHAPTER THREE

ANNA met Todd in a nightclub. She was just seventeen and had never been anywhere quite like it before.

Clubbing had never held any fascination for Anna, but it was the birthday of one of her classmates at the exclusive Kensington school she attended, who had insisted on taking five friends to one of London's liveliest clubs.

It was certainly very lively! But the place was packed and very noisy and the flashing strobe lights which were turning all her friends into fast-moving silvery white marionettes were giving Anna a splitting headache. She hadn't been in there for twenty minutes before she found herself wishing that she could go home.

Todd was also at the club under sufferance. His driver, who had been with him since he was well on his way to making his first million, was getting married that weekend, and he had invited Todd to his stag night. At twenty-three, Todd wasn't into either stag nights or heavy drinking, but he'd felt duty-bound to join in with the party, and only hoped his face didn't show his boredom!

Just before midnight, with the thumping music pounding away inside his head, he slipped away unnoticed to catch a few moments of peace and found a discreetly lit bar on the first floor of the building.

Anna was in search of the loo, and once she found it wished she hadn't, because she was confronted with a full-length mirror and quickly became aware that her sophisticated outfit made her look like some experienced big-sister version of herself.

She had borrowed the dress, of course, because her own wardrobe was sadly lacking in most areas. Anna might have been a pupil at a prestigious and expensive London day school, but her father had no idea how young girls wanted to live.

He was an out-of-touch civil servant who spent most of the time locked away in his mote-filled and dingy office in Whitehall; a changed person, so different from the laughing man of Anna's childhood. Anna's mother had been mown down by a drunken driver when Anna was just fourteen, and since then all the light seemed to have gone out of her father's life. He rarely seemed to be home at all. He did not seem able to share his immense grief with his daughter, coping instead by burying himself in his work.

A lofty and somewhat distant intellectual, he cared nothing for high fashion, and what little he knew had convinced him that it was nothing more than an elaborate swindle designed to part young and impressionable girls from their money. Consequently, while Anna received an adequate allowance, it certainly didn't allow her to indulge herself in the outfits which most of her peers owned.

The dress she had borrowed for the evening wasn't something she would have normally chosen, but it obviously did *something* for her, because Anna had never been quite so aware of men ogling her before. It was a short satin slip dress with shoe-string straps which left the creamy skin of her shoulders exposed. The silvery grey silky material clung to her undulating curves like a second skin, and the eyes of most men in the room were out on stalks.

Todd sipped at his tonic water and observed the woman in the tiny, shimmering dress from out of the corner of his eye. *Great* legs, was his first instinctive thought, and then something made him look closer, and he frowned.

Because for all her beauty there was something about her which did not quite add up. She did not look very comfortable in her surroundings, for a start. And any minute now one of those creeps who had been quaffing far more booze than was good for them was going to breathe stale alcohol all over her and try to chat her up. Or worse.

Todd rose to his feet, unaffected by the fact that every woman present was lasciviously undressing him with her eyes.

Except one.

Anna had noticed him, of course. He was so hunky that *everyone* had noticed him! But only a woman who was supremely vain, or extremely confident, would ever have expected a man like that to look at her twice. And she was neither.

And then she blinked as she saw that he was walking purposefully across the bar in her direction.

She actually peered over her shoulder to see if some glamorous female was standing behind her, giving the tall man with the slanted grey eyes a welcoming smile, but there was no one. Only her. She bit her lip.

Todd saw her obvious and innocent confusion and felt the oddest glow of satisfaction as he drew closer to her.

"Hello," he said, in his distinctively deep voice. "You look lost."

"I wish I was," Anna told him frankly. "This place is worse than being in a fireworks factory."

"Oh? Why?" He was amused and showed it; these days he rarely seemed to meet women who said anything original. Most of them just agreed with everything he said!

"Well, all those lights flashing like mad and the music banging loud enough to perforate your eardrums!" Anna looked around her with obvious disapproval. "And I can't *believe* that they charge those ridiculous prices for drinks!"

"You sound as though you shouldn't be here," he observed drily. "Which rather begs the question of why you are."

Anna shrugged. "I came with some friends," she told him, deliberately omitting the prefix "school".

"And they are...?" He looked around.

"Dancing. Downstairs."

"And don't *you* want to dance?" he questioned, thinking that it would be heaven to have her swaying in his arms to the music.

Anna considered the question briefly. She wouldn't have minded dancing with *him*. Not one bit. But did she dare risk taking him back downstairs to the dance floor? He was the best-looking man she had seen all night. Wouldn't the others just leap all over him, like slavering dogs confronted with a bone? "Not really," she shrugged. "It's too crowded."

"A drink, then? Or a coffee, perhaps?"

"Oh, I'd love a coffee," she said fervently. "Do they sell it here?"

He shuddered. "I believe they do a foul brown liquid masquerading as coffee but I know a little expresso bar just around the corner which serves the best coffee in the whole of London. If you're interested, that is?"

Anna hesitated. She had listened and learnt her lessons in personal safety well, and yet some bone-deep instinct told her that she could trust this man.

"Bring along a chaperon, if it makes you happier," he prompted gently as he correctly interpreted her hesitation.

No fear! Anna shook her head and her bright blonde hair shimmered in the subdued bar lighting. "That won't be necessary—I happen to have a black belt in karate, in case I need protecting."

"Do you really?" he quizzed her in admiration.

"No!" she laughed. "But I had you worried there for a moment, didn't I?"

He laughed back. "Todd Travers," he murmured, and held his hand out.

"Anna Marshall," she told him as they shook hands.

They spent an innocent and absorbing hour over coffee, though afterwards Anna could barely remember what they had talked about. She was glad that she had paid so much attention to all her subjects in class, and also glad that her father had always insisted she read the newspapers thoroughly, because she was more than able to hold her own with the remarkably well-informed Todd Travers.

They stepped out together into the neon-lit street

and he hailed a black cab, then accompanied her back to Knightsbridge. Anna was awfully glad that it was dark, because she started blushing wildly when the driver pulled over outside her building, desperate for Todd to ask to see her again.

Todd had tussled with his conscience during the journey. She was not like the women he usually dated. There was something pure and clean about her which, ironically, made him feel awfully *protective* of her, an emotion he had only ever experienced with his little sister, and his friend from school, Elisabeta. And he had never fancied Elisabeta...

As the cab stopped, his conscience got the better of him, and he forced himself to ask, ''Just how old are you, Anna?''

It was the moment of truth and Anna refused to heed it.

''Twenty,'' she told him blithely, saw his relieved smile, and the die was cast.

During the next few weeks, Anna managed to meet with Todd every single day, while keeping him well away from her father. This proved to be easy since Todd had no desire to share her company with anyone else, and she felt exactly the same about him.

She was evasive when she chose to be, telling him simply that she was on her Easter vacation; when he assumed that she was at university, she let him carry on believing it, justifying it by telling herself that she *would* be at college before long. She, who was normally as honest as the day was long, soon discovered that deception was terribly, terribly easy when you wanted something badly enough.

And Anna wanted Todd...

She didn't care that she was duping him. She had fallen in love with him, but knew that he would drop her like a hot potato if she told him how old she *really* was. And love was love. Anna had already lost her mother; it had made her grow up fast. More than most people she recognised the ephemeral nature of happiness—embraced the idea that you had to grab at it when you got the chance, because you never knew when it might be snatched away from you. She would, she decided, do almost anything to keep Todd Travers in her life...

Todd was in far deeper than he wanted to be too; he had never been in love before either, and it had knocked him for six. For the first time in his life, he was conscious of being in the throes of something much more powerful and much more exciting than reason.

In a way, his life had been as fractured as Anna's. He had inherited a run-down plastics factory in Islington on his eighteenth birthday, and this had played a big part in his decision not to take up a scholarship to Oxford. His father had gambled away what little money the family had left, before running off to Australia and dying penniless just a year later from an excess of alcohol.

It had been left to Todd to support his mother and little sister, and the anger he had felt at his father's betrayal he had channelled into turning the factory into a dynamic and successful business manufacturing luxurious ice-creams made out of the best natural ingredients. It had been a perfectly timed strategy. People were just beginning to rebel against impersonal mass production and were prepared to pay more for quality.

Todd hadn't realised at the time that he was setting a trend, but then he had always been ahead of his time.

Other factories had followed and Todd had diversified. Ailing businesses, seeing his success, had come to him for advice and he'd turned them into profitable companies. In short, he'd made a mint.

Some men, given Todd's physical attributes, would have been tempted to squander a fortune made at such an early age, but he had taken advice from the very best financiers. Before long he was the owner of an impressive portfolio of stocks and shares—the interest alone enough to support him in comfort.

Yes, Todd had worked hard for the last five years—so very hard—and right now he wanted to play...

Making love to Anna became not just a desire but a necessity. The passion he felt for her overwhelmed him, because he hadn't really believed that he would ever feel this way about a woman. His passion was all-consuming. He *had* to have her, in a way which was, initially, much closer to possession than to desire. He felt a primitive need to claim her for his own, to mark her out as his. And if he hadn't been twenty-three and cynical about marriage on account of the way his father had behaved, then he might just have married her anyway...

It was only a matter of time before they ended up in bed together, and only a matter of time before Anna could no longer put off the moment she had been dreading and was forced to tell Todd that not only was she seventeen but she was pregnant, too...

"Darling?"

Anna looked up, disorientated for a moment as she

found herself back in the present with Todd standing in front of her, a cup of tea steaming away in his hand.

"You looked miles away," he observed as he handed her the cup and perched down on the window ledge, stretching his long legs in front of him, the denim of his jeans so faded that it looked almost white. It was dark outside the uncurtained window. Street-lamps dazzled like topaz through the bare branches of the trees which lined the Knightsbridge square. Through the milky haze of a scudding cloud, a sliver of silvery moon could just be detected.

Anna tried and failed to imagine a view other than the one she knew and adored, and tried to repress the shudder which was crawling up her spine. "Where are the girls?" she asked.

"Having their juice and biscuits, and watching children's television. I told them we were talking, and asked them to give us a little time alone together."

"I see." Her voice was curiously flat, and she spoke with none of her usual bubbling enthusiasm.

Todd watched her from between slanted lids. "Drink your tea," he said carefully.

She tried a smile, but it seemed to have frozen her lips into a grimace. "There's no need to treat me like an invalid, you know," she told him.

His eyes narrowed fractionally. "Isn't there? Doesn't one walk on eggshells where invalids are concerned? Carefully avoiding any mention of subjects you know might upset them?"

She put her cup of tea down, afraid that her hand might jump and she would spill it. "Is that why you've sprung this on me out of the blue?" she asked him carefully.

Had he? She had a point. But over the weeks he *had* been dropping hints that all was not well—hints that Anna had not heard, or had simply chosen to overlook. No matter... What mattered was now. How could he compensate for the apparent suddenness of his suggestion? How could he put his vision to her so that she would embrace it enthusiastically, instead of looking at him as though he were suggesting a one-way ticket to Mars?

"This idea of mine—of selling up and moving out. The Americans call it 'downshifting'," he said thoughtfully. "Shifting your life down a gear or two in order to improve it. It means to stop chasing your tail all the time. Can't you imagine *that*, Anna?"

Anna felt as though someone had tipped a bucket of ice over her head. Was that how he saw their life? As a constant race? A trap, even? Like hamsters running round and round a wheel in a cage? Or were they running in parallel existences with Anna smug and secure in her own little world, never realising that Todd was desperately unhappy in his?

"I'm not sure that I can imagine *you* living a life like that," she answered slowly.

"Meaning?"

"Just that you've always revelled in the cut and thrust of city living, of making money, of rising to the top of the pile. The powerful businessman in the silk shirt and Italian suit."

"Maybe that's how I *used* to look at it," he admitted wryly. "But situations don't stay static, Anna. I want to spend more time with you and the girls."

She opened her eyes very wide in surprise. "You do?"

"Yes, I do. Because if we don't change and evolve, then we don't grow."

"You're talking about personal growth, I presume?" she fired at him, thinking that they sounded as though they were about to bring out a new self-help book!

He sent her a rueful glance, and Anna suddenly noticed how incredibly *weary* he looked, with shadows highlighting the sculpted beauty of his cheekbones. She felt another rush of longing. She yearned to stroke that dark, wayward strand of hair from where it had fallen onto his forehead, to ease all the strain away from his broad shoulders with the tips of her fingers. "I guess I am," he murmured.

"And if we don't change? What then?"

The silence which followed her tentative questions stretched out before them like a tightly drawn violin string. "I just know that I don't want to carry on like this, Anna," he told her finally. "Caught up in the frenetic rat race of the big city."

"And the girls?"

"I think they're ready for a change, too. Why don't you ask them?"

"Oh, I will, Todd. Don't worry. I will."

She waited until bath-time to broach the subject, and by then felt that she had regained a little of her usual composure.

The triplets were now ten, but at bath-time they usually regressed to only half those years! There was a huge corner bath in the larger of the two bathrooms and sometimes, like tonight, Anna let all three of them jump in together.

"But no splashing!" she warned them, knowing that the order was ineffectual as soon as she made it.

She let them giggle and blow bubbles and generally wear themselves out for a bit.

"Daddy says you're mad-keen for a horse, Tally," she ventured casually as she tipped water over the newly washed curls of her oldest triplet.

She saw the unspoken, cautious look which passed between three pairs of deep sapphire eyes so like her own, and it reinforced her awareness of their almost telepathic closeness.

It really was the oddest sensation being the mother of triplets, since sometimes she felt that they could exist perfectly well as their own, small, perfectly contained unit, without any interference from herself or Todd. To some extent, Anna was always aware that she *could* have ended up feeling a bit of an outsider, and her determination not to was what motivated her to be so involved in her daughters' lives. Except that Todd was now implying that she had become a little *too* involved.

"Oh, Mummy—I'd *love* a horse! But I'm not asking you or Daddy to buy it. I've saved up enough money from the Premium campaign to buy my *own*!" said Tally proudly, with the air of someone who had practised saying something over and over.

"Yes, I know you have," agreed Anna calmly. She squirted a squeaky toy at Tina, their scatty, youngest daughter, who blinked and then giggled.

"Me, Mummy!" begged Tasha, who was usually the most serious of the three. *"Me!"*

She squirted them relentlessly, until they begged for mercy, and it wasn't until she had them all wrapped up in fluffy lemon bath-sheets, watching while she wiped away the suds from the side of the bath, that she felt confident enough to broach the subject of their modelling.

"And Daddy also tells me you've all had enough of the Premium campaign," she stated bluntly, and then looked at them questioningly.

Again, that same assessing look passed between the three and Anna started to feel that she was the only member of the family who wasn't in on this conspiracy!

"I have," said Tally, very cautiously. "They won't let me ride a horse because it's dangerous!"

"And I have, too," said Tasha. "Because I want more time to study Greek."

"*Greek?*"

"My teacher says she thinks I have a future in Classics," said Tasha smugly, ignoring the chorus of "Sad!" from her siblings.

"And what about you, Tina?" asked Anna gently.

Tina shrugged, and the gesture made her look so like her father that Anna's heart turned over. "I'm bored with being on telly," she told her mother simply.

"*Bored?*" repeated Anna incredulously.

Tina nodded. "There's so much standing around waiting, and then we have to do each take over and over again. And people at school are jealous and keep making snide comments."

"I see," said Anna slowly, wondering just how many other worms were going to come out of the woodwork that day. "And just how long have you been feeling like this, Tina?"

"Can't remember," said Tina evasively.

"Tell me," urged Anna softly.

"Since Grandad died, I guess," whispered Tina.

And Anna nodded, understanding immediately.

Her father, once he had sold the old family home to her and Todd, had moved into a smaller apartment just around the corner. The birth of his granddaughters had brought him to life again, and had made him the enthusiastic man that Anna remembered from her childhood. He had relinquished some of the punishing hours he put in at Whitehall, and had involved himself with the girls as much as possible.

He had spent many happy hours playing with them and making them laugh, watching them grow with pride and more than a little sadness, since Tally in particular had reminded him of his late wife. Later, he had taken great delight in seeing their faces on hoardings all over the country, and on television screens at tea-time.

He had died suddenly but peacefully in his sleep just under a year ago, and through her own grief, and that of the girls, Anna had been acutely conscious of an era coming to an end. Had Todd felt this, too? Had her father's death been the catalyst for him to analyse the quality of his own life?

"Grandad used to love watching your adverts," said Anna gently. "He was terribly proud of you all."

Tasha nodded, deadly serious for a moment. "I know he was, Mummy. But he also said that we should only ever do it as long as we were enjoying it."

"And you no longer enjoy it?"

The triplets held their breath.

"No!" they told her in fervent unison.

Anna smiled. There was no arguing with something as unequivocal as that! "And has Daddy mentioned that he would like to move out of London? Go and live somewhere where we could have more space? Where Tally *could* have her horse?"

Tally's small fists were white as she clenched them together against her chest, the look of longing on her heart-shaped face almost unbearable. "*Could* we, Mummy?" she asked. "Oh, *could* we?"

Anna looked from Tasha to Tina. "Do you both feel the same?"

She saw the indecision which crossed their faces and guessed that they were afraid of appearing disloyal. "Honestly," she urged them. "I won't know unless you tell me. Would you like to move out of London?"

"Well, yes, Mummy. Yes! Actually, we would."

She put them to bed, and read them a story aloud. Several of their schoolfriends had apparently scoffed that they were too old for this most childish of treats, but the triplets held firm. Mummy read so well, and with such funny accents, that she made all the characters in the books come alive for them.

It was past nine by the time she had tucked them up, tidied the bathroom and deposited various forgotten socks in the linen basket.

She wandered back into the sitting room to find Todd stretched out on the sofa, his eyes closed as the peaceful sounds of Chopin drifted exquisitely through the air. His lashes made two soft and sooty arcs, and the sculpted symmetry of his cheekbones cast alluring shadows on his face.

With the hint of a new beard making him appear elementally masculine, he looked for all the world like a highwayman, thought Anna, with a sudden lurching of her heart. As if he had simply leapt from a horse, discarding a dark and swirling cloak, and decided to take a nap right here on her sofa...

He opened his eyes as she walked in, and fixed her with a questioning look.

"Everything okay?" he queried as he saw the sudden tension around her shoulders.

She had already decided that she was going to handle this like an adult, even if she felt like hurling herself to the floor of the sitting room, drumming her heels on the carpet and howling at the top of her voice!

She drew a deep breath. "I think that maybe you're right, Todd," she told him calmly. "I've thought about it carefully, and I think that a change will do us all some good."

Todd sat up in surprise. He had been anticipating all kinds of objections to his idea, certainly not such an easy capitulation. "You *do*?"

Anna's temper was already frayed, and if Todd carried on making out that she was Mrs Unreasonable, then all her good intentions about behaving like an adult would go straight out of the window! "Well, what were you expecting?" she demanded waspishly. "That I would cross my arms with indignation and adamantly refuse to go?"

"Some women would," he observed wryly.

Maybe they would, she thought; maybe they would. But she had already irrevocably changed the direction of Todd's life by becoming pregnant. Did she really have the right to dictate the terms of their future?

"And you naturally thought that I would be among their number, did you?" she probed. "Do you really know so little about me as a woman, Todd?"

There was a moment's silence while he acknowledged the slur on his judgement with a graceful nod of his dark head. "I've known you as a schoolgirl," he stated eventually, in a soft voice which, nonetheless, filled Anna with an odd, uneasy feeling. "Then full and ripe with our children."

He smiled, but it was a smile tinged with sadness. "And after that you became a mother. So maybe you're right. My experience of you purely as a woman has been constrained by all the demands of our instant family. I haven't really known *you* without all the baggage that goes with being a mother who was barely out of her own gymslip—"

"Please don't use emotive phrases like *that*, Todd!" she howled. "It's such a cliché!"

"But it's true, isn't it?" he demanded hotly. "*Isn't* it?"

"And you want to make me feel guilty about falling into bed with you, do you? Guilty about trapping you into a marriage that we were both far too young for? Is that it?"

"Oh, Anna," he whispered, in a strained voice which sounded positively exhausted. "If there is any guilt to be shouldered, then it is mine. I was older than you and much more experienced. I should have seen what I was getting into—hell, I *did* see what I was getting into, but I arrogantly chose to ignore it. I was too blinded by—"

"Lust?" she put in tartly.

He had been about to use the word "love", but

Anna's cynical response killed it stone-dead and it remained unsaid. He looked at her with a chilly grey gaze. "If you like," he agreed evenly.

Anna's hands were shaking as she re-tied the velvet ribbon which held all her blonde hair back in a big, floppy bow. Her back was aching with stress and tension. It had been a fraught and emotional afternoon, one way and another.

His eyes swept over her curved body. Most women would have changed, and yet she still wore the same old leggings she'd had on this afternoon, and the baggy tee-shirt she had hurriedly pulled back on was now splattered with drying soapsuds. Her cheeks were pink and shiny from where the bath steam had obviously given her a miniature facial sauna. Not a single scrap of make-up adorned her face and she looked younger than her twenty-eight years. She was as unlike the cool sophisticates he met every day in his working life as it was possible to be.

And yet still he ached to possess her.

"Why don't you come over here?" he suggested silkily, their wounding words forgotten as desire trickled insistent fingers hotly across his skin. "And take something off—the way you did this afternoon."

But Anna did not feel up to re-creating her uncharacteristic role as siren. She felt racked with uncertainties as she looked at the outrageously sexy face of her husband. Was this the thin edge of the wedge, she wondered, this sudden voicing of discontent? Were ten years with one woman too much? Particularly a woman you had clearly never intended to marry in the first place...

She stared at him, as if seeing him objectively for

the first time in ages. "Not now, Todd," she told him, more coldly than she meant to. "I don't think that our differences are going to be solved by you taking me to bed every time we air them, do you? Or is giving me an orgasm just your way of shutting me up?"

His mouth hardened into a forbidding, stranger's mouth as she spoke with a bluntness he neither liked nor was familiar with. She was deliberately twisting his words, attributing motives to him that he certainly hadn't intended. "Is that how you see sex, then, Anna?" he queried coolly. "As a weapon? A means of getting something that you want?"

"Like I got you, you mean?"

His jaw clenched with anger. She was doing it again—distorting his words so that they ended up sounding like something completely different. "That isn't what I meant, and you know it!" he ground out.

"Do I? It seems that I know very little, as I'm only just discovering. And certainly very little about you, Todd," she responded icily. "For example, I had no idea that you were so desperately unhappy here—"

"Anna—"

"I've let *you* have your say, so please do me the courtesy of allowing me to finish what *I'm* saying!" she gritted out. "Because who knows how many more of your secret desires will come to my attention before this whole business has finished?"

There was an ominous pause.

The expression in his grey eyes made her heart clench with fear. "Finished?" he asked her carefully.

She had meant the business of moving house, but now she saw that Todd had interpreted her words in a different way entirely. He thought that she was talk-

ing about their *marriage*, for heaven's sake! ''Todd, I
didn't mean our relationship!''

But Todd was angry and bitter and disenchanted.
And he feared that one of them was about to say something irrevocable. ''Let's just leave it, Anna,'' came
his faintly bored request. ''Before either one of us says
something that we really *do* regret.''

And he leaned back against the cushions and closed
his eyes dismissively.

CHAPTER FOUR

THAT night, for the first time in their married life, Anna and Todd did not sleep together.

Oh, they had spent nights apart before—when Anna had been in hospital having the girls, and other, thankfully infrequent times when Todd had been away on business trips. But never before had they been under the same roof in different beds.

Anna had showered and gone straight into their room, then lain awake until past midnight while she waited for Todd to join her.

Finally deciding that he must have fallen asleep on the sofa listening to music where she had left him, she padded her way along to the sitting room to find it in darkness, the sofa bare save for a heap of cushions, and her heart froze in alarm.

Where the hell was he? she wondered frantically.

She found out as soon as she pushed open the door of the guest bedroom to see the humped shape of his sleeping form, and her panic turned into a bitter kind of anger.

She allowed herself a brief glance over at the bed. He was sleeping naked; that much was evident. Todd never felt the cold at night, even in the middle of winter, and the sheet was rumpled around down to his bare waist. He had his back to her, one arm sprawled with abandon over his dark, ruffled head, and Anna could see the rock-hard and curved outline of his buttocks through the cotton sheet, as clearly defined as if they hadn't been covered at all...

Rage and desire coursed through her veins like a powerful combination of drugs, and Anna stood hesitantly in the open doorway while she tried to decide what to do.

The sensual side of her wanted to throw back the sheet and climb in next to him and press her naked breasts softly into his back, so that he would give a small, helpless moan of pleasure and start making love to her as he had done so beautifully that afternoon.

And in fact, come to think of it, today's lovemaking had been the most....the most *sensational* she could remember for ages. Was that what disagreements did for you? she wondered half-longingly and half in disgust. Did they make you so hot for each other that you couldn't think straight?

Her mouth thinned as she thought about how manipulative she had been. Deliberately enticing him, seducing him, thinking that he would immediately forget all about moving and come round to her way of thinking.

Which only went to prove how badly she had misjudged the situation.

Get into bed with him? She would sooner get into bed with a cobra!

Turning on her heel, Anna marched straight out of the guest bedroom and Todd slowly expelled the long breath he had been holding since he had awoken to her presence in the room.

And neither of them slept a wink for the rest of the night.

Breakfast was a strained affair. Anna found that she was all fingers and thumbs. She, who could normally cope with cooking three lots of eggs and juggling goodness only knew how many cereal packets, was reduced to a fumblingly bad attempt to feed everyone which only worsened when a sombre-faced Todd walked into the kitchen.

He was wearing a dark suit which matched the shadows beneath his eyes and Anna felt a brief flare of satisfaction as she registered the physical signs that *he* had spent as bad a night as *she*.

She stared into his grey eyes with a totally expressionless face while the triplets chirruped their greetings.

"Hello, Daddy!" said Tally, giving him an enormous smile as she drew an imaginary horse in the air, using her finger as a pencil.

"Morning, Daddy!" Tasha briefly lifted her blonde head from the book of Greek legends she was currently engrossed in.

Only Tina—scatty, impetuous Tina—said what Anna at least was thinking. "Why did you sleep in the guest room last night, Daddy?"

Anna met Todd's gaze over her head and ignored the query in his eyes. *He* had started this, she thought to herself viciously, so let *him* talk his way out of it!

"I've had a slight cold," Todd explained. "And I didn't want to keep your mother awake by snoring."

Tasha, although deeply into her book of ancient legends, still found it impossible to ignore the blatant lack of logic in this statement.

"But what about that time Daddy had terrible flu, *and* a temperature, *and* we had to call the doctor out— he still slept with you then, Mummy, didn't he?"

It was that business of reacting like an adult instead of a child. Unforgivably and unusually, Anna failed the test she had always set herself and involved the children in their squabble. But then they didn't usually have quarrels which felt as serious as this one did.

"Yes, he did, Tasha," she answered her daughter.

"So why, Daddy?" asked Tasha.

"Yes, why, Todd?" queried Anna serenely.

Todd looked furiously at Anna, his eyes spitting hard, angry sparks at her. He turned away to pour himself some coffee, mustering his thoughts, not wanting to say something wounding in front of the girls. Even though, he thought angrily, Anna had clearly had no such qualms about involving them.

He turned back to find four pairs of dark blue eyes fixed on him expectantly. "I've had a lot on my mind just lately," he told them truthfully. "And I knew that I wasn't going to get very much sleep—and so…" he pulled out a chair and sat down, crinkling his grey eyes up at the corners in a special smile reserved for his daughters "…I thought it would be fairer to Mummy not to keep her awake, too. Now put that book down, Tasha, and eat up your cereal."

"Okay," said Tasha easily, and picked up her spoon, the subject forgotten.

Not so for Anna. Her stomach felt like an unset jelly and a nameless dread reached out its cold, dank fingers to envelop her. "Come on, girls!" she said, in a voice intended to be bright but which ended up sounding shrill and empty. ''Go and get your bags together. Your games kits are in the hall. Hurry up, Tina, *please*, darling—we have to leave in fifteen minutes flat!''

The triplets exited the kitchen babbling excitedly, so that once they had gone the silence they left behind proved almost deafening.

Todd poured himself a second cup of coffee and watched Anna while he drank it. ''So what are your plans for today?'' he asked calmly, extracting a slice of wholemeal toast from the rack and spreading it with butter.

So he wasn't even going to *mention* the separate rooms, thought Anna indignantly. Didn't he consider it important enough to discuss—or was this simply the next stage in their marriage? That rows should culminate in segregated sleeping and not be resolved at all. Anna took refuge in clearing away the empty cereal bowls. Anything was better than having to stare into the sombre grey eyes of her husband.

''Oh, just the usual,'' she told him. ''Tidying the flat, changing the linen on all the beds.'' Which would now include the spare room. Unless, of course, he was planning to take up permanent residence there, in which case she wouldn't bother. Though she couldn't quite bring herself to ask him. Not at the moment. ''The girls have a photo-shoot after school for Premium's new, easy-read-label promotion, so I'll be taking them to that.''

''Can you meet me for lunch?'' he asked evenly.

Anna's hand paused only momentarily as it hovered over the dishwasher she was stacking. ''Lunch?'' she echoed, and looked up at him in surprise.

Was it her imagination, or did he look suddenly discomfited?

"Is that such a bizarre invitation, then?" he quizzed softly.

Anna shrugged. "A little. You don't usually ask me to meet you for lunch." But then he didn't *usually* sleep in the spare room, did he? Or suggest that they uproot the family. Or make love to her in a way that, while being wholly sensational in the physical sense, also filled her with a sense of trepidation, because he had seemed so very *angry*, even as he was gasping out his own fulfilment.

"I thought that women enjoyed being asked out by their husbands," he mused.

"Well, you're the one with the experience of women, Todd," she said nastily. "So I expect you're right. Where? And at what time?"

Todd bit back the desire to wipe that haughty and proud expression from her face in the most elemental way possible. To have her vulnerable and soft and sighing beneath him. To wipe out the bitter words and bad feelings with the hard thrust of his body...

The phone rang and dissolved his libido as surely as if he had stood beneath the icy jets of a cold shower. He grabbed at it like a lifeline.

"Todd Travers," he grated, his whole demeanour altering as he listened to the voice at the other end. "Oh, hi, Lucy! No, no, no—of course I haven't taken early retirement! I'm just leaving." He listened. "Oh, did he? No, no, that's okay. Tell him that I'll see him at eleven." He looked down at his wrist, where his costly watch gleamed like the silvery skin of a fish. "You're in very early, I must say," he commented, then put his head to one side and laughed at the response he received.

"No, of *course* I'm not complaining! I'll see you just as soon as I can, but don't hold your breath! I overslept this morning, so I'm bound to hit the traffic." He put the phone down and faced his wife with an unconsciously wary expression, as if he had sensed her silent outrage.

"So who's Lucy?" Anna demanded, even though she loathed herself for sounding like a stereotypically jealous harpy.

He met her accusing stare. "Lucy is my temporary secretary," he told her steadily. "Except that she's so good I'm hoping that I might be able to persuade her to stay."

"Well, you'll have no worries there, will you, Todd? Since we all know about your *particular* powers of persuasion."

He didn't move a muscle. "You're referring to sex, are you, Anna?"

She didn't answer. She didn't dare.

"Are you really implying that I intend to take my secretary to bed in order to get her to stay?" he challenged steadily.

Still she didn't answer. No words would form.

"Because it's a cheap and childish accusation," he drawled cuttingly. "And as well as being inaccurate it's misdirected, because *you* were the one who suddenly started playing the entirely new role of *femme fatale* yesterday afternoon, weren't you, Anna? What were you imagining? That after a little bit of uninhibited lovemaking I'd be agreeing to everything you wanted?"

He rose to his feet, so tall and, for once, so terribly intimidating. "Well, if that was the case then you were completely wrong, sweetheart." He picked his car keys up from the hook next to the giant turquoise fridge he had had shipped over from the States. "It seems that a talk about our future is long overdue, and a restaurant seems as neutral a venue as anywhere. I'll book a table for one o'clock. If you can't or don't want to make it, then let me know."

Fear became anger. She clutched a box of cornflakes to her chest like a talisman. "Why? What will you do? Will you take Lucy instead?"

He paused, his hand on the door handle, a thin smile doing nothing to disguise the disdain in his eyes. "Right at this moment, Anna," he told her honestly, "I'd favour an uncomplicated bite to eat with my secretary any time!"

And he stormed out, slamming the front door behind him and so failing to hear the sound of breaking china as Anna broke more than the habit of a lifetime and hurled one of her favourite cups against the wall.

After she had taken the girls to school, Anna spent the morning in frenetic activity, stripping the beds as though they were contaminated, and tackling a huge pile of ironing as though it were her life's endeavour.

Twice she went to pick the phone up to ring him, and twice she flounced away from it.

Just *who the hell did he think he was*? she asked herself ineffectually as she sprayed polish and rubbed madly at the pine table in the kitchen. Showing his secretary more respect than his wife! Well, let him take his beloved Lucy out to the restaurant, she thought defiantly. Let him flirt like crazy with her over lunch, and then, and then...

A vivid picture sprang to mind. Of Todd plying and being plied with wine. Of Lucy—who in Anna's imagination had the body of a Californian beach babe and an intellect the size of Texas—switching the office phone off and getting down to the serious business of...

Anna picked the phone up and punched out the number of Todd's direct line. It was picked up on the second ring.

"Just bin it," he was saying. "I won't waste my time on it. Hello?"

Anna felt as nervous as she had done on their first date together, when he had taken her to see an art-house movie and they had spent the entire film wrapped in each other's arms, like teenagers. But then she had been a teenager at the time, so maybe it wasn't that surprising. "T-Todd?"

"Anna," he responded cautiously.

"Who were you speaking to?"

Did she imagine his impatient sigh? "To Lucy, of course. My secretary. Remember—I told you?"

"Yes, of course." Anna's mind drifted uncomfortably as she wondered how old Lucy was. The name didn't exactly conjure up an image of a comfortably built, middle-aged dynamo—which was what his *last* secretary had been like. Lucy sounded languorous, lascivious even.

"Anna? Are you still there?"

"Yes, I'm still here."

"Can you make lunch?"

"If you still want me to."

Now she definitely *wasn't* imagining an impatient sigh.

"Of course I want you to, otherwise I wouldn't have asked you, would I?"

"I suppose not," she responded glumly.

"Right. I'll book a table at Orsino's."

A flattering choice, thought Anna, since Orsino's was the flavour of the month—the capital's hottest and buzziest restaurant. "Are you sure you'll get a table at such short notice?" she wanted to know.

"Yes, sweetheart. Meet me in there at one. Okay?"

"Okay. Todd—"

"What?"

"Don't be late." She should have explained. Told him that she would be a bundle of nerves if she was left sitting alone in a flash restaurant. But her request sounded like more of the same stuff she had subjected him to that morning. Jealous harpy.

"No, Anna," he answered wearily. "I won't be late."

She put the phone down and then dashed straight into the bathroom for a record-breakingly fast shower, berating herself for being so prickly with him and wondering why her smoothly run life should suddenly appear to be disintegrating.

Next, she frantically blasted her hair with the hair-dryer and cursed softly for not allowing herself longer to get ready. She could have left the beds until to-morrow—no one would have minded. No one would even have noticed, if she was perfectly honest. It had been a wry observation made by Anna very early on in her married life that, no matter how hard you worked, no one ever gave you any plaudits for doing the housework!

She put on a clean bra and knickers, then took the knickers off again to replace them with another, lacier pair. It wasn't as though she was expecting anything to *happen* during or after lunch, but the pale blue briefs the triplets had bought her last Mother's Day, with ''Save the Whale' emblazoned all over the bottom, didn't exactly make her feel very *sexy*! And sexy was what she wanted to feel today.

Mind you... She twisted her head over her shoulder to catch a glimpse of her rear view, then wished she hadn't bothered. She *looked* like the whale the girls had been beseeching her to save! The black lace of the knickers was cutting in uncomfortably around her hips, and the elastic on the back of her bra looked as though it was about to give up the ghost and snap! She knew she ought to weigh herself, but frankly she didn't dare.

When had she last taken a good look at herself?

How had all these extra kilos managed to creep on without her noticing?

Maybe it was because her period was due. That *must* be it! And that would explain her horrible, bloated appearance, too. And the fact that she had been so mean and nasty to Todd.

But Anna knew that she was fooling herself. She had gained a few extra pounds after the triplets had been born, and she had never really lost them. And then last Christmas Todd had taken all of them to visit his sister in America, where Anna had become addicted to maple syrup and pancakes, with a corresponding weight gain.

So what the hell was she going to *wear*?

She hunted around in her wardrobe with the fervour of someone who had spent all night queuing for the January sales, but nothing sprang out and announced "Wear me!". Well, one outfit did—a finely knitted dress in aquamarine silk—but she couldn't even pull it down over her bottom, and she threw it onto the bed with an expression of dismay.

If she had had more time she could have rushed out to the shops and bought something new, but she didn't really have the inclination, even if she had had the time.

She settled for a short black pleated skirt and wished she had time to move the button so it didn't cut into her waist quite so much. But at least it showed her legs, and her legs had always been—and still were— her best feature. On the top she wore a big cashmere sweater in primrose-yellow, which hid a multitude of sins.

And let's face it, she thought, with a disconsolate look in the mirror, *you're* a frumpy, lumpy, middle-aged housewife. In fact, you look exactly like the kind of unthreatening woman you would like to see working for Todd!

Outside it was drizzling relentlessly. A fine mist of grey rain descended like a dank and impenetrable curtain. Anna struggled to put her umbrella up, but not before the rain had covered her blonde hair with miniature droplets, and she cursed beneath her breath. She had left it loose because that was how Todd liked it best, but now it would go all frizzy and she would end up looking as though she had been holding her finger in the light socket!

Because it was raining, the demand for taxis was high, and by the time Anna actually saw the welcoming amber light of a vacant vehicle the roads were filling up with lunchtime traffic, and she got to the restaurant exactly twenty-five minutes late.

Not that she should have bothered worrying. As soon as she followed the *maître d'* into the discreetly expensive dining room, she saw that Todd was being well catered for in a way which had absolutely nothing to do with food.

A woman on the table next to his, who looked as though she must have depleted the entire world stock of silicone to provide herself with such an enormous pair of breasts, was leaning across and chatting animatedly to Anna's husband.

While Todd listened to her with a benign smile on his face.

The woman's companion was also female, with thick, shiny hair the colour of orange marmalade and tawny eyes which were gazing with open lust at Todd.

Anna unconsciously lifted her shoulders back and began to walk across the crowded restaurant, acutely aware of the skirt cutting painfully into her waist.

Todd saw her and immediately rose to his feet, a welcoming smile on his lips, but a smile which, nonetheless, held a trace of restraint.

He studied her dispassionately as she walked towards him. Apart from the lush bloom that childbirth had given her, she had altered very little in the ten years they had been together, he thought. That pale lemon sweater she wore suited her delicate colouring, and with her hair loose and flowing all the way down her back and the merest hint of make-up on her milky pale skin she looked no different from the girl he had first seen in that terrible nightclub, all those years ago.

"Hello, sweetheart." He smiled, and kissed her on both cheeks.

The two women looked up at the two of them, their mouths gaping wide open, which gave them the unattractive look of two stranded fish, thought Anna maliciously. "Aren't you going to introduce me to your friends, Todd?" she heard herself saying tartly, and then could have kicked herself when she saw the responding smirks of the two women. Such a prissy little request, making it sound as though she was *jealous*, for heaven's sake! Of *them*!

Because if she was being completely honest she didn't really believe for a moment that Todd was contemplating infidelity, did she? And if he *was*, surely he would have gone for a more ravishing and discreet-looking duo than these two!

Then she caught a glimpse of herself in the tinted mirrors which lined the walls, and her heart missed a beat.

Why *wouldn't* he be attracted to women like that, when faced with the alternative? *She*, as his wife, certainly wasn't setting an unreachable standard of beauty and desirability, now, was she?

"Darling?" She looked at her husband expectantly.

"Certainly," responded Todd smoothly. "Delia Pardoe and Maggie Manson—meet my wife, Anna Travers."

Anna didn't need to be the most perceptive person in the world to register the swift look of shock which passed between the two women as they leaned over to shake hands with her. But then perhaps they had imagined that a man as powerful and as rich and sexy as Todd Travers would be married to someone who looked as though she had stepped straight from the glossy pages of a fashion magazine.

A million light years removed from the image that *she* was currently presenting.

"Hi, Anna," said Delia, who was the one with the breasts. "Pleased to meet you."

"Likewise," drawled Maggie, who smelt faintly of cigarette smoke.

Anna cleared her throat. "Hello," she said, trying and failing to inject a little enthusiasm into her voice.

"Delia and Maggie work for Wicken Advertising," put in Todd quickly. "I went to school with their boss, Oliver Wicken—remember, you met him in France last summer, Anna? We go back years and years—"

"There's no need to make us sound so ancient, Todd!" scolded Maggie familiarly, giving Anna a conspiratorial wink as she pulled a pack of cigarettes from her leather handbag. "Is he always like this, Anna?"

"Like what?" asked Anna bluntly.

"Oh, nothing. It doesn't matter!" said Maggie hastily, and slanted her eyes at Delia in a warning expression, before withdrawing an extra-long cigarette from the pack and lighting it.

"Sit down, sweetheart," said Todd quietly, with a smile which Anna *definitely* thought was forced, and she slid into the seat opposite him, trying not to look too dejected. Did he always come to restaurants like this at lunchtime, with clearly available women dripping all over him? It appalled her to think how little she knew of this part of his life—the part which didn't involve her in any way.

Still, at least the two women were drinking their coffee and would soon be leaving, thought Anna, with relief. Their presence was inhibiting, to say the least!

"Like a drink first?" he asked as a waiter hovered.

Someone who had struggled to get into every item of clothing they possessed would have sensibly ordered a diet drink or a soda, but Anna was not in the mood to be sensible.

"White wine, please," she told him firmly.

The wine was brought to the table unobtrusively— cold and delicious and fruity. Anna felt she could have slugged the whole glass down in one, but she had never sought answers in the bottom of a bottle, so she sipped it delicately instead, and fixed him with an expectant look.

"Shall we decide what we want to eat first?" asked Todd, finding that he was as reluctant as hell to start talking. Damnation! If he had been worried about his wife's reaction to moving, he suspected that would be nothing compared to her response to today's little bombshell.

Anna shrugged, sensing his unwillingness to talk, and finding that it matched her own feelings perfectly. "Why not?"

The women on the next table got up to leave as Anna pored over the menu, and she gave them a cool smile of farewell.

She was wavering between the duck and the monkfish when she felt a sharp cramp stabbing at the base of her stomach, and screwed up her face in distress. "Ouch!"

"What's up?" queried Todd instantly.

She shook her head. "Just a tummy ache. It's nothing."

"Sure? Is it your period?"

"I—I'm not sure," she admitted. The weeks and months flew by so quickly these days that she had trouble keeping track of her menstrual cycle.

He tipped his head to one side, his face concerned, and Anna was reminded with a pang of all the times he had fussed over her when she *did* have a period. Bringing her cups of tea and old-fashioned hot-water bottles, and rubbing the small of her back until she began to wriggle luxuriously, like a cat. "Will you excuse me for a minute?" she whispered. "You order for me, Todd—you know what I like."

"Okay," he nodded, and stood up and watched his wife thoughtfully as she picked her way across the restaurant.

It was a predictably fancy and flatteringly lit powder room, with a mirrored ante-room containing vast vases of scented flowers, and various lotions and potions neatly lined up in glass-stoppered bottles. Anna had left the flat in such a tearing hurry that she had completely forgotten to use any perfume—and Todd loved it when she was wearing scent.

She found a light, citrus-based fragrance and sprayed it liberally on the pulse points of her wrists and neck. Sniffing appreciatively, she put the bottle down, and was pushing open the door into the washroom itself when a shrill and vaguely familiar voice halted her in her tracks.

"I just couldn't *believe* it! Did you see the size of her?"

Anna froze stock-still with the awful inevitability of what was coming next.

"I know. Imagine Todd—*Todd*, of all people—being married to someone like that!"

"And how *could* she wear that yellow jumper? If *I* had a backside that size, I'd steer clear of anything other than plain black. It made her look like a huge, wobbly custard! Someone should tell her."

"No wonder he's got a roving eye!" Anna recognised Delia's voice and her skin turned to ice.

"Who? Not Todd, surely?"

"Mmm! *Definitely!* I could have him in my bed at the drop of a hat if I gave him the old come-on!"

"So why haven't you?" Maggie's voice was suspicious.

"What—date a married man? You must be joking! There's no future in that kind of affair, kiddo—they have to be on the brink of divorce for *me* to be interested!"

"Well, now that you've seen her, does that change your mind?"

There was a muffled comment which Anna couldn't quite make out, followed by a shout of laughter.

Beads of sweat formed on her forehead as she recognised her predicament. She was desperate for the loo, but couldn't possibly go in there *now*, in case they realised that she had been listening in to their conversation. Not that she cared what they thought of her eavesdropping. She simply couldn't bear to face them, with them knowing she had overheard every cruel and spiteful thing they had said about her.

She slipped out of the ante-room, then went straight back in again, making a huge noise of pushing open the door to the washroom, while whistling loudly and tunelessly to herself.

Delia and Maggie looked up as she walked in, and both looked faintly embarrassed. Maggie even had the grace to blush, noticed Anna with some satisfaction as she set her face into a superior little smile.

"Hello *again*!" said Delia insincerely.

"Oh, hi," said Anna, looking faintly bored as she headed for the cubicle, and the two women beat the hastiest retreat she'd ever seen.

She waited until she had recovered some of her composure before heading back to the restaurant, and that was when the reality of her situation hit her, hard. She had been aware for some weeks now that things between her and Todd weren't perfect, that something had changed, but now she had to face up to the fact that they were somehow far worse than she had imagined.

Did Todd have a roving eye? She would have bet her wedding ring that he didn't, and yet how could she be so certain? What did she really know about what he got up to in the course of a working day? Or with whom? She, who had never had a paid job in her life, but had channelled all her energies into bringing up the triplets.

Whereas Todd inhabited a completely different world outside the home they shared, a world of which she rarely caught a glimpse.

One thing she *did* know was that she didn't dare think too deeply about some of the damning things she had overheard Delia saying. Not right now. Not when she had to go back into that crowded restaurant and face her husband without breaking down and crumbling into a useless heap in front of him.

Anna felt as though she was walking back to their table in slow motion, the strange ringing in her ears deadening the sounds of the other diners, and the only thing she could register was the unmistakable air of disquiet which glinted in Todd's grey eyes.

When she reached their table, he was already on his feet. "Good heavens, sweetheart," he frowned. "Are you quite sure you're okay? You look awfully pale."

Should she tell him what she had just overheard? Challenge him with it in the middle of a busy and crowded restaurant? Would Todd not just accuse her of listening to idle gossip?

Meanwhile, just the mention of it would probably be enough to have her in floods of insecure tears, and she wanted—no, *needed*—to stay calm. She would bring it up later, when she was feeling less vulnerable and emotional, and they would probably have a good laugh about it together.

"I'm fine now," she said, and forced a smile as she took her seat. "Did you order?"

"Mmm. Tomato and avocado salad, then skate wings in black butter. I hope that suits?"

"Lovely," she murmured politely, thinking that they sounded like strangers meeting for the first time. But maybe it *was* a little like that, in a way. They so rarely had a treat like this—lunch together in a fancy restaurant. Usually she was far too wrapped up in her life with the triplets. There always seemed so much to do, and not enough hours in the day in which to do it. Not just taking them to photo-shoots, but also to the numerous ballet and singing and acting classes which their agent had recommended.

She wondered just why this unexpected lunch was turning out to be less of a treat and more of an endurance test.

Grey eyes were narrowed piercingly in her direction. "Anna, is something wrong? You look awfully tired."

"Well, maybe that's because I *am* tired!" she shot back, even though she had vowed on the way over not to ruin the meal by starting an argument. She didn't feel she could face *another* night of sleeping on her own! "I had a pile of ironing as high as Everest this morning, and the girls left the flat in the most disgusting state."

"Like I said yesterday—if you run round after them all the time," he commented wryly, "how on earth are they going to learn to do it for themselves?"

"I won't make them do household chores when their lives are already so busy!" she defended herself fiercely, before realising that she had added more fuel to Todd's argument. "Maybe you should try telling them that they'll have more time to spend on tidying their rooms when they give up their Premium campaign—*then* let them see if they're so keen to stop working! And will you please stop looking at me that way, Todd?"

"What way is that?" he murmured, his eyes darkening like the night.

"As though you'd like to…to…"

"To?" he put in helpfully.

"To take me to bed!" she whispered in a shocked voice.

"Well, I would. I like it when you're trying to be angry with me and you get all heated and wave your hands around. It makes your breasts move so spectacularly and so enticingly that I long to peel that sweater right off and feast my eyes and my hands on them. Right now."

Her eyes widened with shock as well as pleasure, her nipples tingling in response to his open admiration, the encounter in the washroom temporarily forgotten as she felt the syrupy unfurling of desire render her as weak as a kitten.

She patted her hot cheeks with the palms of her hands. Just what had got into Todd lately? she wondered in bewilderment. He was usually so controlled— a master of self-restraint, with every action thought through before it was acted upon. "Well, don't! Not here! We're in the middle of a public room and it's very distracting."

He shifted uncomfortably in his seat and gave her a wry smile. "Damned right it is! Change the subject, Anna!"

She remembered how he had looked yesterday afternoon, when he had come home unexpectedly and taken her to bed. A vision of his sleek and powerful nakedness swam before Anna's eyes, and she felt even weaker. "I can't remember what we were t-talking about in the first place," she stumbled.

"Your arduous morning doing housework." He shrugged dismissively, then wished he hadn't when he saw the look on her face.

"There's no need to make it sound so inconsequential!" she snapped. "That *is* what I do, after all!"

Todd rested his chin in his hand and studied her.

"But you don't have to! I don't know why you won't let me employ someone to help you around the flat," he objected, with the air of a man who had said the same thing over and over again, so many times that he ended up sounding bored rigid with the whole subject.

And the boredom wounded Anna more than anything else he could have said or done, because it attacked her where she was at her most vulnerable. It was the image of herself that she loathed— a boring, stay-at-home housewife. And yet it was the truth, wasn't it? "You know *why*! Because I don't go out to work."

"And what does that have to do with anything?"

"It means that by doing all the housework and chaperoning the triplets," she told him candidly, "at least I feel as though I'm contributing something to the household."

"Is that why you seem so reluctant for the girls to stop modelling?" he questioned slowly. "Because their work justifies your existence?"

Anna thought that there were kinder ways he could have put it. "Maybe," she admitted. "Though I certainly didn't think about it consciously in those terms."

He leant back in his chair and surveyed her thoughtfully from between narrowed eyes.

"And anyway," she continued passionately, warming to her original theme, "why on earth *should* I employ someone else to do what I am perfectly capable of doing myself? And just what am I supposed to do while the flat is being cleaned? Sit around like a princess and watch the cleaner while I file my nails?"

Todd sipped his wine as the waiter put plates of neatly sliced tomato and avocado in front of them, determined not to rise to her provocative comments. The last thing he wanted was to rile Anna any more than she would be riled when she discovered what he was about to tell her...

Grey eyes were intent on her. "You could think about starting a career for yourself."

"Like *what*?" she demanded tartly.

She sounded so disgruntled that he decided to try another tack. "Or you could try doing what other wives of rich men do," he suggested silkily.

"What? Become a lady who lunches? Or sits on charity committees? Or shops till she drops?" Anna shook her blonde head in indignation, oblivious to the sizzling glance the head waiter sent in her direction. "Unless—" and she put her fork down on her salad plate and stared at him with clear blue eyes "—unless you're advocating that I start doing what the *really* rich and bored get up to."

"Which is?" he prompted softly.

"Have an affair," she mouthed at him, and saw his face whiten, although he must have *known* she was speaking hypothetically. Mustn't he? "Oh, don't worry, Todd—I wouldn't *dream* of opting for that option. I hate to disillusion you, but I'm just not that kind of woman."

"Then what kind of woman are you?" he teased, trying to lighten the mood, to bring her out of herself. Wanting to catch a glimpse of her slow, infectious smile which had definitely not been much in evidence today.

But Anna's self-esteem had been punctured too

deeply for teasing. "I honestly don't know," she told him seriously. "I've submerged myself so much in domesticity and for so long that I don't think I know who the real Anna Travers is."

"Well, I do," he murmured.

She idly pushed an oil-covered basil leaf round and round the plate, and stared at him. "You do?"

"Sure I do. She's a mother," he said softly. "The best mother in the whole darned universe! And an amazing wife, of course—"

"No, I'm not! And there's no 'of course' about it!" Anna shook her head in denial, then fiercely pushed a strand of golden hair away from her face. Amazing wives were slim and accomplished and sexily assertive in bed. And she was none of those things. Why, her attempt to seduce him yesterday had been nothing more erotic than the removal of one very baggy sweater that was long past its sell-by date! Todd had removed everything else. "I may be the first," she told him proudly. "But I'm certainly not the second!"

"I think that *I* should be the judge of that, don't you, Anna?" he quizzed gently. "And in fact it's given me a brilliant idea about what you *can* do with your life when—*if*," he amended, catching the warning glint in her eyes, "they *do* give up the Premium campaign."

"Oh?" she queried, curious in spite of herself.

"Mmm. You can lie around wearing nothing but outrageous pieces of lingerie, waiting for your husband to return from work at odd hours of the day so that he can make mad, passionate love to you," he suggested wickedly.

"Like yesterday, you mean?"

"Oh, I think we can improve on yesterday," he promised, on a sultry note. "Don't you?"

Anna began to pleat the linen napkin on her lap nervously as she tried to visualise what her ample curves would look like, bursting out of the tiny scraps of lace she imagined that Todd had in mind. "Who on earth would want to m-make love to someone who looks like a b-big, w-wobbly custard?" she asked him quietly, in a voice which sounded suspiciously close to tears.

He sat back in his chair again and gave her a look of utter bafflement. "A *what*?" he demanded.

"You heard me!"

"I'm not denying that—but you might as well be speaking in tongues for all the sense you're making, Anna."

Her voice quavered even more. "M-maybe it's time to give you the freedom to do what you *really* want to do!"

His sceptical look intensified. Maybe her period *was* due—he had rarely seen her so emotional. "And what's that, sweetheart?"

Now he was patronising her. "M-make love to Delia whatever-her-name-was!"

There was a moment of angry silence before he levelled his eyes at her in a furious grey stare. "Delia Pardoe, you mean?" he clipped out stonily.

"Of course I mean Delia Pardoe! How many Delias do you know, for goodness' sake?"

"I think you'd better elaborate, don't you?" came his cold response. "Since I don't have the slightest idea what you're talking about."

"I'm talking about *her*, of course! Delia Pardoe!
And you! You wanting to make mad, passionate love
to *her*! I overheard her telling Maggie, just now, in
the loo!''

"Did you?"

"Yes, I did!"

"And you believed her?" he queried, in an icy
voice. "Naturally?"

Well, she hadn't. That was the point. But maybe
that was because she hadn't *wanted* to believe it. And
some trouble-making imp inside her made her refuse
to tell Todd that.

Because Anna was feeling fat and frumpy, and at
that moment she couldn't imagine *any* man wanting
her, let alone a man like Todd. Her ego was severely
wounded and so she struck out. She looked fixedly
down at her lap, not wanting him to see the tears
which were welling up in her blue eyes. "How should
I know what to believe?" she whispered. "Why on
earth would she want to lie—particularly as she didn't
even know I was listening?"

His mouth hardened and he made a contemptuous
little sound beneath his breath which Anna had never
heard him use before and which only intensified her
earlier feelings of drifting apart from him. And of isolation.

"I didn't bring you here today to discuss the fantasies of a woman I barely know," he said dismissively.

"No? Then what did you bring me here to discuss?
There are a number of topics on the agenda, aren't
there, Todd? Like why you didn't come to bed last

night and slept in the spare room! Why don't we discuss that?''

A muscle worked in his cheek. ''I thought my reasons for that were fairly obvious. I felt that we were going to say some pretty wounding things to one another unless we gave each other a little space.''

''Except that we still seem to be saying wounding things to one another today—so clearly your strategy didn't work, did it?'' she retorted flippantly.

''No. But it was worth a try.'' He refilled her wine glass, slightly surprised at the speed with which she had drunk the last, but then he had drunk more than usual himself.

Anna was beginning to feel woozy. All that unaccustomed wine on an empty stomach. She forced herself to swallow down some avocado, then looked up at him, at those brilliant grey eyes which seemed so terribly distant and disapproving right now. ''So, Todd.'' She sucked in a deep breath. ''What's on the agenda? Did you want to talk about moving again? Was that why you brought me here?''

He shook his head. ''I have no intention of bombarding you with propaganda just to get you round to my viewpoint, Anna. I asked you to think about moving, and I'm assuming that as a reasonable person you'll do just that.''

''Well, I hope your assumptions don't disappoint you,'' she muttered darkly.

''But that wasn't the reason I asked you here today,'' he said slowly.

''No.'' She straightened her back and waited.

''I have to go away,'' he said suddenly.

''Go *away*?'' There was something terrifying about

the way he just came out with it, and Anna stared at him across the restaurant table, her widened eyes looking intensely blue, as dark and as blue as the deepest ocean. "Go where, for heaven's sake?"

"To Romania." He dragged the words out as if he were pulling teeth. "I'm afraid that Elisabeta is in trouble."

CHAPTER FIVE

IT WAS completely illogical, since Anna knew Todd well enough to know that he would not tell her in such a cowardly fashion, but when he had said "go" like that she had been convinced that he meant he was about to leave her. So that when he'd followed it up with the statement about Elisabeta her overriding emotion had been one of huge relief.

Which only lasted as long as it took for his words to sink in.

She narrowed her eyes at him. "What do you mean—Elisabeta's in trouble?"

Todd sat choosing his words with all the care of a diplomat. He had done everything in his power to keep the peace between his wife and his oldest friend, but the two women had never really hit it off as well as he would have liked, despite the fundamentally innocent nature of the long-standing friendship.

His relationship with Elisabeta had always been close—he had known the dark-eyed Romanian girl since they were both thirteen. They had attended the same fairly progressive, co-educational boarding-school, and had become firm friends—mainly, Todd suspected, because he was the only male in their year who had not fallen headlong into love with her! Elisabeta had been lonely and frightened, confused by a language and set of customs she was unfamiliar with, while Todd—with a younger sister who adored him— was a naturally protective person. And, more importantly, he was confident enough to have no hang-ups about being friends with a girl.

He had helped Elisabeta with her English—and her maths—and in return she had hero-worshipped him and made him laugh, both of which had appealed hugely to the rapidly growing teenage Todd, who by fifteen was already taller than most of his teachers.

Later, at seventeen, they had kissed experimentally at the school's end-of-year dance, but there had been nothing more, since that had been all that either of them had wanted, though for different reasons—Todd because he simply couldn't imagine Elisabeta in the role of lover, and Elisabeta because she had no intention of being one in a long line of Todd Travers's women, to be discarded when she had outgrown her use to him!

But because they were often seen so happily in each other's company their schoolfriends had always confidently assumed that Elisabeta and Todd would end up married one day—they seemed so perfectly suited. And it had to be said that on long evenings when some wannabe blonde bimbo had been boring him rigid Todd had even given the topic some thought himself.

Until he'd met and fallen in love with Anna...

"What *kind* of trouble?" Anna asked tartly now, taking his words at face value. "Are you trying to tell me that Elisabeta's pregnant?"

Todd looked shocked. "Pregnant?" he echoed. "*Elisabeta?* But she isn't even married!"

That was rich, thought Anna, coming from Mr

Shotgun Wedding himself! But then Todd had always credited Elisabeta with a certain saintliness that he certainly didn't associate with his wife! Anna counted to ten, but only got as far as six.

"Neither were we!" came her mocking response. "But a wedding certificate isn't mandatory if you want to have sex, Todd, and sex can, and often *does*, result in pregnancy—as we both know only too well!"

The couple at the next table exchanged an amused glance as her words carried, while Todd looked even more shocked. No doubt he hadn't been expecting *this* kind of response when he'd asked his normally quiet wife out for lunch. And Anna might have giggled at the expression on his face had the reason for their disagreement not been troubling her quite so much.

He frowned, his thick, dark brows furrowing together. "Anna, darling, it isn't like you to be quite so—"

"Crude?" she put in helpfully, thinking that, no, it wasn't. But it was certainly very liberating! "Well, how am I supposed to react when you suddenly announce that you're off to Romania to help someone who everyone knows has carried an extremely large and flaming torch for you all these years?"

"That's rubbish!" he snapped. "There has never been anything untoward in my friendship with Elisabeta, not in all these years—as well you know."

Oh, yes—Anna knew *that*! And, in a way, the very innocence of the relationship posed its greatest danger. For how could she ever hope to compete with a woman who remained, apparently, as pure as the driven snow?

Not that Anna actually *disliked* Elisabeta or anything, because she didn't, although Elisabeta was definitely Todd's friend, as opposed to hers. And, what was more, Elisabeta was godmother to Tasha, and all the triplets loved her dearly.

It was just that Todd and Elisabeta went together as well as eggs and bacon, and Anna was nervous about that compatibility. Particularly if he was going to be alone with her, and particularly if he hadn't been getting on so well with his wife...

But wasn't she jumping the gun more than a little? Whoever mentioned competing? She needed to ask herself some very simple questions.

Like, did she or did she not love her husband?

Yes. More than she had imagined she would ever love anyone.

And did love not incorporate total trust?

Yes, it did.

She fixed him with her most interested and most adult smile. "So why the visit?" she questioned brightly. "And why the urgency?"

"Oh, the usual reason." He spread his palms out apologetically, as if it were all his fault. "Money. Or, rather, a shortage of money. Her bank is beginning to run out of patience."

"Oh? I always thought that Elisabeta's family were well-to-do. Aren't they distant descendants of the Romanian royal family or something?"

"Mmm. That's right. But the title doesn't guarantee riches—they were always comparatively impoverished." Todd ate some bread, mightily relieved that Anna seemed to be taking it all so calmly. "What little there was they've spent most of, and are looking around for ways of earning an income."

"But presumably without doing what the rest of us do, and going out to work?"

His grey eyes gleamed. "That's a little unfair, Anna."

"Is it?"

"Elisabeta has been looking after her mother for the past five years—you know how sick she has been. So she hasn't exactly been idle."

"No, I suppose not," agreed Anna reluctantly, thinking that Elisabeta could do no wrong in Todd's eyes.

"And they have a delightful vineyard which has lots of potential, but just needs a shove in the right direction."

"Which only you can provide, I suppose?" She heard the sarcasm distorting her voice, but seemed powerless to halt it.

"I've told them that they need to consult an agricultural expert who specialises in vines," he informed her.

"You seem to have discussed Elisabeta's problems at some length," observed Anna caustically.

He sent her a bemused look. "But you know that we talk on the phone from time to time, sweetheart."

Not from home he didn't, Anna thought grimly.

He was not foolish enough to take her silence as interest, but felt an urgent need to fill it somehow. "Plus there's no glass for the bottles available in their particular district. Not affordable ones, anyway, and I know a wonderful place in Harlesden which can provide them with—"

"Oh, spare me the details, will you? If I want a short, comprehensive course in wine manufacturing, then I'll go and look it up in the library!'' snapped Anna, seeing his mouth tighten at her abruptness, but not caring.

"You object to me going there; that much is obvious," came his dry rejoinder.

"No, Todd!" Anna had been about to take another gulp of wine, but put the glass back down on the tablecloth instead, her hand was shaking so much. "Although I must confess that I'm not actually over the moon about you flitting off to Romania, what I actually *object* to is having all these things sprung on me—"

"Anna—"

"Please don't interrupt me!" she told him fiercely, and then watched with satisfaction as he closed his mouth in surprise. Of course, he wasn't used to such firm assertion from his wife, but then they usually agreed on things.

Until yesterday.

Anna renewed her attack, her eyes spitting blue sparks at him. "Look at it from my point of view," she challenged fiercely. "In the space of two days you first tell me that you want to completely change our way of living, and then you blithely announce that you're off to Eastern Europe to stay with the saintly Elisabeta!"

"Anna, that isn't very fair—"

"Well, maybe I don't *feel* like being fair!"

"Elisabeta would hate to be described as 'saintly'," he mused, and Anna could have quite happily punched him at that point.

"Just tell me how long you're going to be away for," she said coldly.

"Only a month." He looked at her steadily, his thick lashes almost obscuring the steely grey glitter of his eyes. It was a look which Anna found irresistible, and, what was more, he knew it! How manipulative of him to turn it on at will! Particularly when he was trying to get her to agree to something she was opposed to on principle. "Five weeks at the most."

Five *weeks*!

But Anna forced herself not to react any more than she already had done. There was her pride to think of. Why show how insanely jealous she felt at the prospect of him spending all that time with Elisabeta, however much she trusted Todd, and however much he attempted to convince her that everything was innocent and above board?

Because it couldn't possibly do any good, could it? Other than to create a climate of unease and mistrust. Particularly if he was set on going anyway—which he clearly was.

"I guess I'll just have to hope it's closer to a month," she sighed, pushing her barely touched plate away. She took a large mouthful of wine and nearly choked when she caught a glimpse of her reflection in the rose-tinted mirror behind Todd's head.

The combination of the wine and the heat in the room had given her cheeks an intensely ruddy glow which did not flatter her at all—particularly when contrasted with the yellow sweater which had come in for such cruel criticism. She looked like a flustered canary and her lip wobbled as she set the glass down.

Grey eyes were narrowed in her direction. "What is it, Anna?" he murmured.

"J-just that those women were right!" she wailed.

"Which women?"

"The ones in the loo. Who were talking about me. They were right. I *do* look like a wobbly custard!"

Todd's mouth tightened once more as he came to a quick decision on how to reassure his wife. He stared down at the salad she had hardly touched and at the scant inch of wine left in the bottom of the bottle. If they carried on the way they were going, drinking at this rate at lunchtime, which neither of them was used to, *and* on an empty stomach —then they would both need to be carried out of the restaurant!

"Aren't you hungry?" he growled.

She shook her head muzzily. "No."

"Right!" He stood up and held out his hand decisively. "Come on."

"Where are we going?"

"You'll see," he told her rather forbiddingly as he clasped her hand and began to lead her through the crowded restaurant.

Anna was aware that he briefly stopped to speak quietly into the ear of the *maître d'*, and then suddenly they were outside, in the rather sobering grey drizzle, where Todd hailed a cab and bundled her into it.

"Soho, please!" he barked.

Soho? "Todd, where do you think you're taking—?"

"Be quiet," he growled, and kissed her with a vengeance.

He hadn't kissed her quite like that for years, thought Anna dazedly. Not even yesterday, on the sofa. Not with that sense of urgency which was just this side of desperation. As though he couldn't get enough of her. And the fact that they were in the back of a taxi, with the driver probably watching them through his rear mirror, only added to the piquant thrill that Anna was experiencing.

"Todd!" she gasped deliriously as his hand grazed her acutely sensitised breast which was straining against the soft primrose-coloured sweater. "We can be seen!"

"No, we can't," he murmured confidently into her ear. "I'm shielding you, my darling, though not completely. Because if I was I would be inching my way up your thigh right now, and removing your panties and—"

"Todd!" Her blood felt as thick and as heavy as honey as it thundered in her pulse-points.

His words were barely discernible. "Because I've never made love to you in the back of a cab before, have I, Mrs Travers?"

"N-no," she stumbled, wondering if that was what *most* married couples did—and if that was the case then *their* sex life seemed pretty conventional in comparison! She got a sudden, vivid picture of her and Todd smooching in the taxi with three grizzling and bad-tempered toddlers climbing all over them! "B-but we've never really had the opportunity."

"Would you like me to?" he murmured throatily, bending his head to kiss the base of her neck softly, and Anna almost leapt into the air, so turned on by what he was saying that he might as well have been touching her...

Her head fell back, her eyes closing helplessly, and Todd shot her a narrow-eyed stare of comprehension. Dear Lord, he thought, his eyes darkening with almost unendurable passion. She looked very close to the edge...

Already!

He pulled away from her and she let out a small moan of protest. "Come on, sweetheart," he urged. "Open your eyes. We're almost here."

Dimly, she became aware that they had reached his suite of offices in Soho, and that he was half-lifting her out of the cab, where the fresh air and the rain cooled her down, and reduced some of the livid colour which was flaming in her cheeks.

"Can you try and act normally just for a minute?" he quizzed her. "While I take you up to my office?"

She nodded, not needing to ask what the purpose of her visit to his office was. It was written as plainly as day in his eyes.

He wanted her.

And she wanted *him* right back.

Somehow she managed to get past his secretary, Lucy, who actually looked quite sweet, and his assistants, without raising *too* many eyebrows, but she was blushing as if it was going out of fashion.

"Hold all my calls, please!" called Todd over his shoulder as he pushed her into his office and locked the door behind them.

Their eyes met for only an instant—Anna's full of surprised anticipation, while Todd's were so dark with desire that they glittered like coals.

"Come here," he grated, and, to her everlasting relief, pulled her into his arms and started to rain hard, sweet kisses down on her mouth.

He lifted his head only briefly, in order to peel the yellow sweater over her head and to drop it negligently

by their feet. "Let's get rid of that, shall we?" he
suggested evenly, then he bent his face to hers again,
moving down until his tongue found the line of her
cleavage which spilled out so enticingly over her bra,
tracing a moist path there which promised to take her
to heaven and back.

"Mmm," he sighed, pushing her back against his
oversized desk. His tongue teased one nipple which
poked so provocatively through the fine lace, while his
hands began to hoick her skirt up around her thighs.
"I don't think I want to wait, Anna. Do you?"

Wait? Right now she would sooner *die* than wait!
Anna had always had an extremely satisfying sex life
with her husband, but right now she found herself the
victim of an escalating hunger which was in danger of
spiralling right out of control, because Todd had never
treated her this way before. As though she were some
woman he had just picked up in a bar, instead of the
mother of his children. "Oh, Todd!" she breathed ex-
ultantly, feeling positively *rampant*. "Do that again!"

"What? *That*?"

"Yes! *Yes*! That! Oh, yes, *please*!" was her blissful
response as she gripped the edges of his desk with her
palms.

She heard a rasping sound as Todd struggled to un-
zip his trousers, and then it dawned on her just what
he *did* mean to do! *Here!* On his office desk! Her eyes
widened into disbelieving saucers, and Todd saw her
gaze and correctly interpreted it.

"Yes," he whispered steadily, though his breath
was coming in short, painful bursts. "I know what you
want, Anna. You want me to take you right now and
right here, don't you, sweetheart? You want me to

make you come on my desk, among all my papers. Don't you?'' This as his fingers slipped inside her panties to find her deliciously ready for him.

''Ye-e-e-s...'' She shuddered helplessly as he tugged the panties down over her thighs and then kicked them off.

Todd felt like a man possessed as he pushed her back so that she was lying on the desk, and then, with one of the most elemental surges of passion he had ever experienced, he drove into her eager flesh, so hard and full and supremely powerful that he heard Anna cry out, almost in disbelief.

He closed his eyes briefly as he swayed between ecstasy and despair, the reason for the latter emotion becoming abundantly clear as, for the first time in his life, he found that he was going to be unable to wait much longer...

Anna wanted to savour the moment, to revel in the illicitness of the act, to enjoy the sensation of being ravished on her husband's office desk in the middle of the afternoon! But it was not to be, and she felt almost cheated as she felt her body start to convulse around him. In the fleeting second before undiluted pleasure filled her every sense, she saw his eyes close and heard him give a gasp of disbelief as she felt wave upon wave of delight before he stiffened with his own release.

Todd rested his head on her breasts, his breath warm and rapid on her moist skin, and there was complete silence in the room. Anna had no idea how long it went on for, but it seemed like several minutes before she felt recovered enough to ask him, ''Why did you do that?''

"Didn't you like it?" he teased indistinctly, his mouth pressed up against her lacy bra.

"You kn-know I did," she breathed weakly, and gave an ineffectual little tug at his hair.

He withdrew from her with a small expression of regret. "I could have stayed like that all day," he sighed, before bending to retrieve her panties and kissing her tenderly on the lips before placing them in her hand.

"Why, Todd?" she asked again, wondering what sort of picture she made as she bent to put them on, then located her discarded sweater on the floor over by the window.

He smiled as he watched her. "Pleasure is the *usual* reason," he murmured, but Anna shook her head.

"Don't try to wriggle out of it! That isn't what I meant, and you know it."

His face was suddenly very serious. "You mean, why did I bring you here to my office to make love?" he queried softly.

"Y-yes," Anna gulped, her heart contracting wildly as she relived that swift, overwhelming union. She pulled the yellow sweater over her head, and then shook her hair out, like a dog after it had been left out in the rain.

"Would you rather I had booked a hotel room instead? Is that what you're saying?" he queried. "Well, I would have enjoyed that, too, sweetheart!"

"Please don't change the subject, Todd," she beseeched him in a low voice. "I'm curious."

"Well, so am I. And I have been for some time." There was a long pause as his face assumed a reflective expression. "*Very* curious."

Anna looked at him expectantly, something inexplicable in his tone making her question sound tremulous. "Curious about what?"

His grey eyes grew smoky. "About what it would be like to ravish you here, *and* in a hotel room, come to think of it. About what it would be like to drive you down a remote country lane and have you all to myself, or to ravish you properly in the back of a taxi—"

"Todd!" Anna felt slightly giddy with fear. "What's happened to you all of a sudden?"

"Nothing has happened to me *suddenly*," he told her, with the glimmer of a smile. "I've been feeling this way for some time."

"You sound like some frustrated, sex-starved—"

"No, no, no!" He shook his head in firm denial. "Why on earth would you assume that, Anna?"

"What else am I to assume, when I discover that you've been nurturing erotic fantasies about me? And it seems pretty obvious why! Are you trying to tell me that our sex life gives you no pleasure?"

Todd sighed. "You know perfectly well that it does. Sweetheart, why don't you come over here beside me, and sit down?"

But she stood her ground as the fear of losing him manifested itself in stubbornness. "I don't want to sit down, if it's all the same to you! I want to know what's behind this sudden change of heart."

He perched on the edge of the desk, in the very same position that Anna had been in just moments before, and a dreadful sense of foreboding swamped her, like a cloud.

"Anna, darling," he told her softly. "You are a wonderful lover."

"I could say the same for you!" she returned. "Except that, unlike you, I don't have the necessary experience to make comparisons!"

"Comparisons are odious," he grated. "And besides, you can hardly blame me for having had lovers before I actually met you! Can you?"

No, he was right. She couldn't. But that didn't stop her feeling jealous of all those women who had gone before her.

"It's just that we've never really had the chance to conduct a full courtship," he reminded her softly. "Think about it, Anna."

Anna was silent for a moment while she considered his words. When they had first met, she had been so in love with him and he with her that the moral question of whether or not she should go to bed with him had simply never arisen. It had just *happened*—one blissful afternoon in February soon after their encounter in the nightclub—and it had seemed as right and as inevitable as the rising of the sun each morning.

They had been helped by the fact that the opportunity to fall into bed had been handed to them on a plate. Her father had rarely been at the flat, preferring instead to bury himself in work at his office. Anna wondered if it had ever occurred to him that his little girl might be straying into an adult world unobserved. Or maybe he had just shrugged his shoulders and accepted the inevitable.

When Anna and Todd had finally plucked up courage and gone to see him, to tell him the momentous news that she was pregnant—with Todd holding her firmly by the hand and telling her that, no matter what her father's reaction might be, he would look after her—she had not known what to expect.

But her father's reaction had not been what *either* of them would have predicted. The paternal outrage and shock which Todd had been anticipating had simply not materialised. Anna's father was a widely read intellectual who found that there was very little in the world which surprised him.

He had nodded in that reflective way of his and told them that in some countries girls as young as twelve took husbands! Then he had asked them both in turn, Anna first, if they loved one another, and, on being told ''yes'', had informed them that having children was difficult at the best of times. And that giving birth at seventeen was *not* considered to be the best of times. Also, that he highly recommended that they legitimise the relationship by getting married since it would afford the baby the most protection.

''That's only if you *want* to marry, of course,'' he had added quickly, not wanting to be accused of holding a shotgun to his only daughter's head.

''Oh, but we do,'' Todd had said firmly. ''We do!''

Many twenty-three-year-old men might have felt completely swamped by the way in which events seemed to have overtaken them. But there had never been a moment's hesitation in Todd's mind about what course of action he would take. He had been determined to do the right thing by Anna. ''We *want* to get married. Don't we, darling?''

''Oh, yes,'' Anna had breathed happily, knowing that she would have accepted this beautiful man on any terms he cared to offer. How young she had been!

''It makes everything much simpler,'' Anna's father had added, in his cultured, beautifully modulated tones. ''From a purely legal point of view.''

And, in a bizarre way, both Anna and Todd had felt ever so slightly cheated over her father's eminently reasonable reaction to their news!

Even Todd's mother had accepted their revelation with equanimity, but by that time she and Todd's sister were living in America, and so were a long way from the action.

In a way it had all been too gracefully accepted— a little parental opposition might have kept their youthful rebellion alive! Because, for all her joy at the thought of marrying Todd and bearing his child, Anna had been very aware of the door clanging loudly shut on her carefree youth.

The wedding had been in keeping with what had prompted it. A simple, rather hastily arranged affair at Chelsea register office, in front of Anna's father. Todd's mother and his sister Alana had flown over for the occasion.

Oh, and Elisabeta, Anna remembered grimly. Elisabeta had been there, too.

She had been dressed entirely in black, like a new widow, and Anna could recall the look of disappointment which had clouded her big brown eyes as if it were yesterday.

Anna had worn a white silk dress, so simple as to be almost austere. Her hair had hung like a pale cloud, falling loosely over her shoulders, her only adornment a waxy and fragrant camellia worn above her ear.

''You look like a woman from the South Seas!'' Todd had laughed delightedly, after placing the shiny gold wedding band on her finger and bending his head to kiss her.

"But I left my grass skirt at home!" Anna had giggled, closing her eyes to greet his kiss, though part of the reason was to blot out Elisabeta's hurt white face.

The "reception", such as it was, had been held in a Knightsbridge restaurant close to the flat which Todd had been in the process of buying from Anna's father. It had been a quiet, rather subdued affair, slightly marred by the recent discovery that Anna was expecting not one child, nor even two, but three...

Anna's thoughts drifted back to the present as she became aware that she was caught in the piercing path of Todd's grey gaze.

He stared deep into her eyes. "Don't you agree with me, Anna—that our relationship had a fairly unconventional beginning?"

"You mean that we weren't introduced at a tennis club and didn't date chastely for two years before announcing our engagement?"

He shook his dark hair and shuddered. "God forbid! I can't think of anything worse."

"What, then? What are you trying to say?" And then she stupidly wished that she had instinctively *known* what he was thinking. In the early days they had shared almost everything—including their thoughts. So how had they drifted apart like this? As though they were trying to have a conversation in different languages?

Todd sighed, choosing his words carefully, aware that if relationships were to flourish there had to be communication. He just didn't want to hurt her.

"What I'm *trying* to say, Anna, is that you were a virgin until I came along. In fact, you were the only virgin I'd ever made love to, and, whilst I was immensely honoured, I was always very aware of my responsibility towards you."

"There's no need to make me sound like a waif and stray!" she fired back with indignation. "Just some urchin you'd picked up off the streets!"

He didn't react. "That wasn't what I meant and you know it," he explained patiently.

His grey eyes glittered with uncomfortable memory. "I had to carry the burden of knowing that not only had I taken your virginity, but I had made you pregnant, too!"

Anna couldn't listen to a minute more of this! She waved her hand in front of his eyes in an exaggerated attempt to gain his attention. "Excuse me, Todd; it may just have slipped your mind, but *I* happened to be there, as well! Remember? And I may be a woman—"

"Anna, that's not fair!"

"I may be a woman," she repeated, undaunted, "and I may have been younger than you and less experienced than you, but I am perfectly capable of making my own mind up, thank you very much! And I wanted to go to bed with you just as much as you wanted to go to bed with me!"

He made one final attempt to convince her, because Todd was fully aware of his physical mastery and he had taken full advantage of it with Anna, even though an unlistened-to voice in his head had warned him of her innocence. He had guessed that she was lying about her age, but he had ignored that as well. In fact, he had wanted her so much that he hadn't given a damn about the consequences. ''Well, you were lucky.''

She stared at him, slightly bewildered, until it dawned on her exactly what he meant and then she glared at him. ''Lucky that it happened to be *you* who took my virginity, you mean? Because you happened to be such an ace lover? Why, of all the arrogant statements I've ever heard anyone come out with, that one *has* to take the biscuit!''

''Lucky that you loved me!'' he ground out furiously. ''And that I loved you back! What if I'd been some unspeakable womaniser who had just been looking out for the main chance? What then?''

''Then I wouldn't have fallen in love with you, would I?'' she told him gently. ''Give me *some* credit for a little judgement, Todd!''

He looked fractionally appeased, the hard line of his mouth softening for a moment. ''I do!''

''It doesn't sound like it!''

''Well, I do. It's just that there was no time to get to know one another properly before your pregnancy began to take over. And *how*!''

Anna nodded, recollecting the almost obsessive delight the medical profession had taken in her condition. Spontaneous triplets were rare enough—one in six thousand four hundred, according to her obstetrician. But the fact that she was only seventeen years old had made her pregnancy a real *cause célèbre* at her local hospital. Medical students had clustered in huge groups at the foot of her bed as though they were witnessing the second coming, and Anna had felt like a freak!

"No, that's certainly true," she agreed slowly. "I seemed to spend every available second down at the hospital, having scans! Remember? And every obstetrician in the Southern Hemisphere wanted to feel my bump!"

"And remember when the girls actually arrived?" His voice was soft with emotion, but the huge surge of pride they had both felt at their daughters' safe delivery had not cancelled out the bone-deep fatigue which had taken over both their lives, especially Anna's, during the triplets' first year.

"*Remember* it?" queried Anna wryly. "I remember walking round like a zombie with dark-rimmed eyes. *And* a big tummy which would not go! And there never seemed enough time to spend working out on my figure, the way that the other rich Knightsbridge mums seemed to do."

"That's because you refused point-blank to employ a nanny," he reminded her softly.

Because they had been *her* children, hers and Todd's, and she hadn't believed that anyone could love them the way that they could. And if most of the burden had fallen on Anna while Todd was working, well—so what? Why entrust their precious bundles to a nanny? She had seen some of her friends' nannies— young girls who seemed to care less for the children in their charge than for spending hours trying out different shops with a grizzling youngster in tow. How could someone like that provide the triplets with better care than Anna could?

"Oh, Todd," she sighed. "What a way to start a marriage!"

The memory of her physical appearance still had

the power to make her wince, as did photographs taken
of her at that time. But Todd's desire for her had not
dimmed, even if intimacy had had to be snatched
whenever possible. Which wasn't, she now saw, as
often as *most* newly-weds would have made love. Had
Todd secretly resented having to temper his sexual appetite because they constantly seemed to be sur-
rounded by squawling infants?

She thought of the three girls now, of how independent they all were, compared to those early days.
Regret mingled with satisfaction at how far they had
come, and she felt her eyes growing misty. "How
things have changed," she whispered.

Todd stood up suddenly and took both her hands in
his. His grey eyes were very intent as he looked down
at her. "But there's nothing wrong with that, Anna,"
he murmured, and caressed her palm with the pad of
his thumb. "Change is inevitable—part of life. And
just think of all the endless possibilities for our life
together in the future."

"But your immediate future is taken up with
Elisabeta, isn't it?" Anna reminded him acidly.

His mouth hardened as she stonewalled him yet
again. "I'll try and come back at weekends," he
promised, but his voice was terse and his grey eyes
glittered dangerously as they watched for her reaction.

And Anna felt so emotionally churned up that it was
as much as she could do to tell him not to bother.

CHAPTER SIX

"TODD said *that*?"

Anna bit deep into one of the doughnuts she had brought round to Saskia's gorgeous Chelsea house, and jam squelched out in a ruby-coloured dollop and fell onto her plate.

She looked across the room at her friend, who was sprawled full-length on a scarlet sofa, and whose casting director husband, Russell, had been the first to spot the triplets' potential and launch them on their "Premium" career.

Anna had met Saskia and Russell Goldsmith at school—their son Charlie was in the triplets' class— and the two couples had been friends ever since, occasionally attending first nights at the theatre together, and the exhibitions and concerts for which the ultra-trendy Russell always seemed to be able to get tickets. "He did. He said *exactly* that," Anna echoed gloomily. "He implied that we're in a rut!"

Saskia pursed her lips. At almost six feet tall, with spiky hair the colour of ripe aubergines, she looked exactly like the ex-model she was, except that since giving birth to Charlie she had swapped the catwalk for a camera and discovered that she had a gift for taking photos which told a story all of their own. Now she was in the enviable position of being one of the city's leading photo-journalists; she worked as a free-lance, getting her work into some of the capital's most prestigious publications. "And is Todd right, Anna?" questioned Saskia shrewdly. "Do *you* think you're in a rut?"

Anna had given this question a great deal of thought, especially since Todd's departure for Romania on Sunday evening, after which she had spent the whole night blubbing quietly in her bedroom, muffling her face with the pillow, in case the triplets might hear her.

"No!" she denied immediately, then caught the beady expression in Saskia's eyes and shrugged. "Well, maybe a *bit* of a rut," she admitted reluctantly. "If you mean in the literal sense, then yes, I suppose we *have* been following a fixed pattern of behaviour. Living in the same place, kids settled at the same school."

"But that's *life*!" exclaimed Saskia dramatically. "That's what people *do*! It's also called contentment! What does Todd want to do instead?"

"Swap the city for some rustic dream." Anna stared at her sugary fingers and dropped the remains of her doughnut on the plate as if it were on fire. Why was she eating fried carbohydrate with jam in the centre, for heaven's sake, when she could barely do up the waistband of her skirts already? When two strangers had been reduced to hysteria by the size of her hips and her choice of clothes? "Sloshing around up to his knees in mud," she added gloomily.

"He's obviously having a mid-life crisis!" Saskia declared as she leapt to her green-leather-clad feet and poured them both a cup of expresso.

"That's exactly what *I* told him!" said Anna, even more glumly.

"And what did he say?"

"That he was too young to have a mid-life crisis."

"Well, he *is* only thirty-three," commented Saskia thoughtfully. "So I suppose he does have a point! Mind you, Russell was thirty-three when I met him— it's a very dangerous age for a man," she added darkly, without bothering to clarify her provocative remark.

"Hmm. I suppose so. The trouble is that the girls are on his side." Anna sipped her coffee, thinking that it might not be the best idea in the world to mention that the triplets weren't at all eager to renew their contract with Premium. Certainly not to Saskia. Well, not *yet*, anyway. "Tally wants her own horse and, of course, we could hardly keep it in the communal grounds! And the flat *is* cramped—I know that. Not in terms of space," she added, because she had seen Saskia's disbelieving look, "but simply because we don't have enough rooms. I suggested moving somewhere bigger, but I'm afraid that Todd is tired of London."

She threw Saskia a warning look. "And before you come out with that old chestnut about a man who is tired of London being tired of life—please don't bother! I already quoted it, and Todd just shrugged his shoulders and said in that rather arrogant way he has sometimes that Dr Johnson was talking out of an orifice not usually associated with speech!"

Saskia hid a smile. Along with just about everyone else who met him, she adored Todd Travers! "And where is the great man now?"

"In Romania. Waving his magic wand and helping dearest Elisabeta on her way to becoming a wine tycoon!"

Saskia screwed her eyes up. "You're not jealous of Elisabeta, surely?"

Anna was fed up generally, but most of all she was fed up with being sensible. "Oh, it's such a bizarre idea, I know! I mean, why on *earth* would I be jealous of the fact that my husband is spending a month with a dark-eyed beauty with outstanding brains, who happens to think he's the greatest thing since sliced bread?"

"But there's never been *anything* between Todd and Elisabeta, has there? Honestly?"

No, there hadn't, Anna conceded with a shake of her head. But this new Todd, this Todd who claimed that he wanted change and lots of high-profile sex— who was to say *what* he might want now?

"So how did you leave it with him?" Saskia quizzed, raking her green-varnished fingernails through her short, spiky hair.

"Oh, things were very amicable between us," said Anna slowly. Amicable. What a horrible word! It sounded like the name of a new building society! But she wasn't telling Saskia the whole truth. Because in fact things hadn't been quite as hunky-dory as she would have liked before Todd's departure to Romania.

After several days of uneasy truce following their restaurant lunch, they had been in bed together the night before he had been due to leave, and Todd had reached for her in a lazy way which had set her heart thundering. He had dipped his dark head to her ear and murmured throatily, "Want me?" even as his hands had been working their sweet, sweet magic.

And Anna had gasped, "You know I do!"

She had wanted him and yet had almost despaired of her weakness where he was concerned, wondering why she was always so compliant in Todd's arms. He had just started to kiss her with a thoroughness which left her dizzy when one of the triplets had appeared at the door with a sickly green pallor and they had sprung away from each other, guilty as thieves. Tasha had crawled into bed with them complaining of feeling ill, and had promptly thrown up all over the duvet!

Anna had changed all the bedlinen while Todd carried Tasha into the sitting room, and when she had come back from the utility room she had found the two of them on the sofa where they had fallen fast asleep, white with exhaustion. She had had neither the energy nor the inclination to wake them, so she'd covered them up with a duvet and left them there, then crawled into bed on her own and spent the rest of the night staring gloomily at the ceiling. So much for a romantic farewell!

Todd had shrugged and silently mouthed "Sorry!" at her over the breakfast table, but Anna hadn't been able to conjure up more than a weak smile. She *knew* that their disastrous last night had been no one's *fault*, and certainly not Todd's, but, coming as it had at the end of a bad week, she had felt short-changed and unsettled at the thought of him going out to Elisabeta when so many things lay unresolved between them.

"I've promised him that I'll think about moving," Anna added reluctantly. "While he's away."

Saskia raised her eyebrows. "And what else are you planning to do while he's away?"

Anna stood up and wandered over to the window, where the cherry blossom was heaped in candy-coloured drifts on the branches of the trees. She turned round and caught an unexpected glimpse of herself in the huge mirror which hung over the fireplace, and shuddered.

Her blonde hair hung all the way down her back, in the same style she had worn it in for the last ten years. The night she had met Todd it had looked exactly the same, only in better condition! That morning she had put on a big overshirt in blue denim which matched her eyes. It looked pretty good when teamed with her crisp white cotton trousers and it hid a multitude of sins, but suddenly Anna discovered that effective camouflage was no longer enough to boost her self esteem. She was only twenty-eight years old, for heaven's sake, and she was dressing like a pregnant woman! She wanted to start wearing outrageously trendy clothes while she was still young enough to do so!

"I'm going on a diet!" she announced, immediately realising from Saskia's lack of protest that she should have done something about it a long time ago. "And I'm going to have my hair cut!" she added recklessly. "Seeing as it's looked the same for the last I don't know how many years!"

"What? Does Todd know?"

"I do not have to go and obtain written permission from my husband every time I wish to make a change in my life!" Anna returned, with dignity. It couldn't be one rule for him and another for her—and he had gone off to Elisabeta's side without asking *her* if she minded!

"He's the one that made me look at myself and realise that maybe I *am* in a rut," Anna continued. "So he can hardly complain if I decide I'm going to do something about it. In fact, I'm going to completely change my image!"

"Are you, now?" Saskia sprang up from the sofa with a grace which belied her gangling height and began to look Anna up and down. "Have you got a leotard?" she questioned thoughtfully.

Anna gave her a look of mild surprise. "A leotard? Yes, I think I have. Somewhere," she added as she recalled a brief burst of enthusiasm for keep-fit which had flourished shortly after the birth of the girls, and had withered with similar speed once she had succumbed to total exhaustion! "But it's not beyond the realms of possibility that I might buy another. Why?"

Saskia smiled. "Mind if I take a few photos of you along the way?"

Anna screwed her eyes up suspiciously. "Of *me*? In a leotard? What for? As a "before' poster for a slimming campaign?"

"As a photographic record of your progress. Who knows? We might even be able to do something with it."

"Like what?"

"Don't jump the gun, Anna," Saskia smiled blandly. "Just get round here tomorrow wearing the thing, and I'll take a few snaps. I have an idea that might work—but just let me check it out with Russell before I tell you."

"Okay," Anna shrugged, thinking that she would

go straight home to the fridge and eradicate all the chocolate ice-cream. And then she imagined the triplets' reaction to that, when they returned home from school.

No, she thought regretfully. Simply removing temptation was not the answer to gaining control of her life, especially since temptation lay almost everywhere! No, if she wanted to lose weight she was going to have to follow a sensible diet, combine it with regular exercise and use lots and lots of the dreaded "W" word.

Will-power!

Tina opened her blue eyes very wide. "Mummy, why aren't you eating anything?"

Aware of the upsurge of anorexia among schoolgirls, and conscious of her duty to coach her three daughters in healthy eating patterns, Anna shook her head vehemently. "I *am* eating, darling. I'm eating plenty—*you've* seen what I put away at mealtimes!"

Tasha pulled a face. "Plenty of carrots."

"And carrots are very good for you," smiled Anna.

"And celery!" piped up Tally, who was just putting horse stickers all over the front of her new school folder. "You're always eating celery!"

"Celery fills me up and is extremely nutritious," explained Anna patiently.

"I'd rather have a chocolate biscuit!" Tina winced.

"Well, to be perfectly truthful, darling, so would I," admitted Anna, with a smile. "But I don't do the amount of sport that you girls do, so I'm not burning the biscuit off!"

"Burning?" Tina looked confused and immediately started sniffing the air. "What's burning?"

Anna burst out laughing. "It's all to do with the units of heat required to give us energy—I expect you'll learn about it in your science lessons soon."

"I can hardly wait!" Tina grimaced. "How come you know so much about it—is it that gym you've joined?"

"It is," nodded Anna, thinking of the courage it had taken her to take out membership of a club which was full of people with the most perfect bodies imaginable. "They have a class for people who want to lose weight as well as tone their bodies up, and so I've been going to that."

Tasha looked up from her book with interest. "Does Daddy know you've joined?"

Anna shook her head. "No, he doesn't. And I don't want any of you to tell him! I want it to be a surprise for him."

Tally made the sound of a horse trotting. "When *is* Daddy coming home?"

Tricky. Anna resolutely took a sip of her black coffee, trying, as Saskia had urged her, to enjoy the strong rich taste, instead of immediately wishing that she could add cream and sugar to it! "I don't know exactly. He's hoping to come home at the weekend—"

"Hoping?" Tally squeaked with disappointment.

"Well, yes," Anna nodded, giving her oldest daughter a comforting squeeze. Of the three girls, Natalia was the one who most resembled Todd in character and when her father was away she missed him like mad. But then, so did Anna. She wondered if he was missing her in the same way... "Elisabeta and her family are in a spot of bother and they're very short of money.''

"So why couldn't Daddy just *give* Elisabeta some money, then, Mummy? Then he wouldn't have to go away, would he? And he's got loads and loads of money, hasn't he?''

"That isn't the answer,'' answered Anna severely. "This is a long-term problem which needs to be sorted out properly. If someone's hard-up, you can't just keep handing money out to them willy-nilly. That's just treating the symptoms instead of tackling the root cause of the problem.''

A loud shrill noise began to echo through the flat and Anna's heart raced with excitement. "There's the phone! Quick! It might be Daddy,'' she added, listening to their excited squeals as the three of them ran towards the nearest phone. "And don't forget—Mummy's get-fit campaign is a secret, okay?''

Tina stopped, and turned slowly around to survey her mother. The youngest and scattiest of the triplets, she was also the most sensitive. "But I don't like secrets, Mummy,'' she scowled.

"A surprise, then,'' Anna amended. "It'll be a nice surprise for Daddy when he comes home to find that I look less like a rice pudding and more like—''

"Like who?'' asked Tina innocently.

Anna shrugged. She wasn't sure, really, just who she wanted to look like; she was only certain what she *didn't* want to resemble, and that was a lumpy yellow custard!

While the girls were speaking to their father, she stole a quick look at herself in the mirror. *Had* there been a change in her physical appearance after only one week? She pulled her baggy sweatshirt tight, so that it showed her figure.

Her stomach certainly seemed to bulge less, that was for sure—although Anna wasn't sure whether the fifty sit-ups she did daily were responsible, or if it had anything to do with the steamed fish and plain vegetables which she had been consuming for supper night after night.

And it was only when she'd cut out biscuits completely that she'd realised how often she had relied on them to give her an instant energy-giving fix of sugar. But, of course, there was no nutritional value in a biscuit, as her personal trainer had told her very sternly. No wonder she had felt tired so much of the time. She had already begun to feel excited about what Todd was going to think of his new, energised wife!

She had also wanted to cut her hair into a completely different style straight away, in order to change how she looked in a big, *big* way, but Saskia had persuaded her not to—or rather Saskia's husband Russell had.

Russell was the archetypal casting director—smooth and handsome, in a denim-jacketed, longish hair kind of way, and invariably spot-on when it came to physical appearance. He had narrowed his baby-blue eyes and subjected Anna to a long and assessing look which, to be perfectly honest, if it had come from anyone other than her best friend's husband, she might have considered rather insulting.

"Let's wait to see the shape of your face *without* all that puppy fat before we decide on a hairstyle," he had told her, quite seriously, and then wondered why Anna had aimed a mock-punch at his solar plexus!

"Mummy!" yelled Tasha now, and Anna jumped guiltily away from the mirror. "Daddy wants to speak to you!"

"I'm on my way!" she called back.

Anna waited until all three girls had chatted to their father, and then she shooed them all away, feeling oddly shy—but then he had been gone just over a week, and the only other time they had spoken on the phone, just after he'd arrived, he had sounded indistinct and a long way away.

She had hoped that he might ring her every night, but the lines to the farm had been down—a common complaint, according to Todd. Very convenient, she had thought tartly, but had bitten her lip and not said so, because she certainly didn't want to come over as some jealous old harridan—not when he was so far away from her.

Anna had tried very hard not to dwell on what kind of time he must be having on a beautiful and isolated Romanian estate with a woman who was so stunning that the world and his wife were always wondering just why she had never married. While Anna herself had never wished to question too closely the reason why...

She picked up the telephone tentatively. "Todd?"

"Hello, darling," came the familiar deep, rich voice, "How are things with you?"

How curiously formal these long-distance phone calls always sounded, thought Anna. Because you couldn't hope to fill in the minutiae of daily life which made up most of everyday conversation, so instead you came out with bizarre, stilted replies like, "I'm fine, thanks, darling. How are you?" Now why hadn't she just come out and told him that she loved him and missed him? Was it because she was waiting for a similar declaration from *him*?

"Mmm, everything's great—much better than I expected! I've found a source of good, cheap glass wine bottles in Germany, which sounds extremely promising. I'm planning to fly over there tomorrow, to investigate the possibility of using them to bottle the estate wine!"

It was the last thing she wanted to hear. Todd sounded more exuberant than she had heard him in a long time. But then he was basically reorganising Elisabeta's life—in response to a doe-eyed look of gratitude, no doubt. What man *wouldn't* be flattered at being placed in such an unequivocally powerful role by a woman of Elisabeta's calibre?

"That sounds exciting," she responded woodenly.

There was a pause and the line crackled. "Not really what I'd call *exciting*, sweetheart. It's a fairly short turnaround, and factories in the heart of industrial Germany are not in the parts of the country which usually attract sightseers!"

"Oh." Now why had she clammed up? Why couldn't she think of a single darned thing to say? Was it because she didn't want to bore him with tales of the girls' frenetic round of activities or the fact that the latest shoot for the Premium campaign had had to be cancelled, due to bad weather? Was she loath to relate this to him, in view of his opposition to the triplets' career and his desire to end it as soon as he could? Or was it simply because, at times like this, she felt as dull as ditchwater?

There was a loud crackle. "Are you still there, Anna?"

"Yes. Yes, I'm still here."

"Do you fancy coming out to Germany with me?" he asked suddenly. "You could fly in from London and I could meet you there."

If she hadn't been feeling so insecure, she might not have been so irritable and said something so unforgivable. "Well, that's hardly the invitation of the century, is it, Todd? You paint the bleakest picture imaginable of your proposed trip to Germany, and then you suggest that I join you. Great! And just what am I supposed to do with the girls in the meantime?"

Todd's voice sounded equally irritated. "It's hardly an insurmountable problem! You could have them looked after. That's never been a problem before. Alternatively, you could bring them with you—"

"What? To a—"

"Oh, forget it, Anna," he said wearily. "Forget it! It was just a suggestion. I thought you might enjoy the change. That's all." There was a muffled shout at the other end of the line and then some kind of muffled response from Todd. His voice, when he spoke again, sounded vaguely apologetic, and Anna's heart picked up frightening speed. "Listen, sweetheart, I have to go—supper's just about ready."

"And I suppose Elisabeta's cooking it?"

"Elisabeta is giving her sick mother her medication," he told her coldly, a frown appearing between his dark brows as he wondered what on earth was happening to the two of them. "I'll ring you in a couple of days—you might be in a slightly better mood by then."

"Don't bother!" snarled Anna, and slammed the phone down hard on him—something, she realised with a sinking heart, that she had never done before, not in all the time she had known him.

She went through all the motions of helping the girls with their homework, and putting them to bed, but she felt as though a dark spectre was lurking in her heart.

And, try as she might, she couldn't shake off the persistent image of Todd pouring his heart out to Elisabeta about the unreasonable attitude of his wife.

Even worse was the thought of just *how* Elisabeta might be comforting him in return...

CHAPTER SEVEN

ANNA spent the next three weeks dramatically redefining herself. And, in a way, it was good that she had some project of her own with which to fill the suddenly empty hours. Because, with Todd away, an enormous gap had appeared in her life.

Suddenly her whole existence seemed to have lost its focus.

Not only was there no other adult to cook for in the evenings, but there was no welcoming sound of his key in the lock either—a sound which invariably still made her sit up with a mixture of excitement and expectation as she waited for the first sign of his gorgeous face. Even after all these years...

Television programmes she might normally have enjoyed, simply because she would have watched and discussed them with Todd, now seemed dull and unwatchable. Even books that she had put off reading because she had never seemed to have the time before no longer held any allure. She tried, but the sentences danced like hieroglyphics before her eyes—devoid of all meaning. And how on earth could you concentrate on the plot of a book when all you could think of was how much you missed your husband?

Oh, Todd had been away on business trips before, but never for this long. And never with another woman, Anna reminded herself acidly. Plus they had had that row on the phone, when she had cut the connection. Anna had rung back the following evening to apologise and Todd had assured her that it was forgotten, but their subsequent conversation had been decidedly stilted. If she hadn't had the girls to focus on, she didn't know what she would have done. And *that* made her think about what it would be like as the girls grew more and more independent and, inevitably, moved away from both her and Todd.

And what would she be then? The kind of woman she suspected that both she and Todd would despise? Nothing but the bored wife of a very rich man?

Not if she could help it!

But at least the fears which lurked at the back of her mind provided Anna with an incentive to change the areas of her life with which she was unhappy. In fact, she began to get quite excited about Saskia's idea of photographing her progress as she struggled to get fit.

"I really think there's a book in this, Anna," Saskia told her one day, when she called round mid-morning to find Anna religiously performing press-ups on the sitting-room carpet, with a cooling cup of herb tea on the coffee table beside her. "Or, rather, *Russell* thinks there is!"

Beetroot-faced and shiny from her exertions, Anna collapsed onto the carpet with a strangled puff. "Book? What are you talking about?"

"These." Saskia spread out a handful of glossy black and white photos in front of her. "Look."

Anna looked and then almost fainted with horror as the overriding image of an enormous dimpled bottom in clinging Lycra jumped out at her, like a giant map of the moon.

"Oh, my God," she moaned in horror. "It's *enormous*!"

"What is?"

"My *bottom*, for heaven's sake!"

"Your bottom is not *enormous*," said Saskia patiently. "It's just slightly curvier than normal."

"No, it isn't!"

"Just because the media always project an unrealistically skinny image of womanhood, which is impossible for most women to attain, *doesn't* mean to say you should keep putting yourself down!"

"Destroy them, for heaven's sake, Saskia," moaned Anna. "Destroy them, please!"

"Well, Russell says they're fantastic!" Saskia defended her work.

"Then Russell must have a very warped perception of what fantastic *is*," answered Anna moodily. "Though I suppose fantastic *can* mean grotesque, so maybe he's accurate, even if he isn't right!"

Saskia picked up the photographs and deposited them safely back in their envelope, before following Anna out into the kitchen where she sat watching while Anna poured out two large glasses of mineral water, and handed her one. "Thanks," Saskia said, raising her glass.

"You're very welcome!" Anna murmured, her eyes glinting with sardonic humour.

Saskia sipped at her drink and put the glass down on the breakfast bar. "But seriously, Anna," she said, waving the envelope around with the air of someone who had come fully expecting to do battle. "I happen to think that these pics have got great potential!"

"The potential to do what? To make people feel ill?"

"Don't be so negative!"

"Oh, please! If *your* bottom was that wide, then *you'd* be negative!" Anna stared deeply into the fizzing bubbles of her mineral water as though she were staring into a crystal ball.

Saskia shrugged. "Admittedly, your bum *does* look a little on the large side in those first shots I did of you—"

"More like the width of the Grand Canyon, you mean?" interjected Anna gloomily. "Rather than 'a little on the large side'!"

"But just take a peep at *these*!" Saskia withdrew another batch from the envelope she was holding. "See! Look at the difference just three weeks can make!"

Anna actually found herself speechless as she looked closely at the photographs Saskia was holding. Not that she was suddenly confronted with an image of the next great supermodel. Far from it, since Anna was neither tall enough nor leggy enough, nor naturally skinny enough, to join forces with *that* particular breed.

But there was no doubt at all in her mind that three weeks could make an *enormous* difference. Enormous being the operative word! The step classes and the celery and the swimming had all combined to shave off the dreaded "love-handles' which had taken up residence on her hips, and because her stomach and abdomen were much flatter her newly firmed breasts looked much larger in comparison.

"See what I mean?"

"I *do* look better," admitted Anna, staring closely at each picture in turn, as though her eyes were deceiving her.

"You look *amazing*!"

Saskia smiled. "You should have heard Russell raving on about them, and he's no pushover! Now, about this book—"

But Anna shook her head. "Let's be realistic for a minute, shall we, Saskia? A few photos of me looking less like a whale than usual are hardly going to make a book, now, are they?"

"Well, Russell thinks they will—and he's in the business. Let's face it, Anna—you're a woman with a high*ish* profile—"

"The triplets are the ones with the profile," Anna corrected her sagely. "Not me. They're the Premium children."

"But we sell you as their *mother*! The Premium *woman*! Facing the same problems that thousands of other women face. Women will be able to identify with you, Anna. You're pretty but not overtly so—and certainly not threateningly so."

Which sounded like a back-handed compliment! "Go on," said Anna, interested now, in spite of her reservations.

"Women are fed up with role models they have nothing in common with!" Saskia went on. "Teenage beanpoles who look in need of a good, square meal—or some minor actress type who has decided to jump on the fitness bandwagon. Whereas *you*, as a woman who has had three children—''

''Born all at the same time, don't forget!'' interjected Anna, infected now by Saskia's enthusiasm.

''Exactly! Well, if *you* can get your stomach looking as flat as an ironing-board, then you'll inspire other women to do the same!''

''You'd have to get Premium to agree, wouldn't you?'' Anna frowned thoughtfully as the idea sparked into life.

''Russell's already spoken to them.''

''He *has*?''

''He has. And they're dead keen on the idea. Dead keen. Especially if we can manage to knock up a few recipes featuring their products and throw those in, too!''

''*Recipes?*'' squeaked Anna. ''What recipes?''

''The ones you always manage to throw together— dummy! I know you make a hobby out of putting yourself down, Anna, but you're surely not going to deny that you're a brilliant cook, are you? How about that prawn and courgette thing you do so well—*that's* low in calories as well as being very good for you, isn't it?''

''Well, ye-es,'' responded Anna doubtfully. ''I suppose it is. And you can serve it with salad or roasted vegetables, instead of rice or bread, which makes it even lower.''

''Brilliant! And have you got any more like that?''

Anna shrugged. ''Well, there's my stir-fried chicken thingy, with cashew nuts and spinach—''

''Great!'' Saskia rolled her eyes like a mime artist. ''Russell goes *crazy* for cashew nuts!''

What Russell did or didn't like seemed beside the point, but Anna refrained from saying so. "Of course, you'd have to restrict the number of cashew nuts if you wanted to reduce your calorie intake."

"Of course!" Saskia nodded eagerly and carried on looking at Anna with expectation.

"And there's my black-eyed beans with mushrooms, of course—"

"Get writing those recipes down!" purred Saskia. She topped up her glass of mineral water and raised it in a toast. "I think we're onto a winner here!"

Todd rang that evening and Anna rushed to the telephone, eager to hear the sound of his voice but, more importantly, eager to find out when he was coming home to her. His sombre tone stopped her in her tracks.

"Anna..."

Her heart felt like a lift which had plummeted out of control as fears spilled helplessly into her mind about why he should say her name in that serious, frightening way. "What is it?" she demanded, alarmed.

"It's Elisabeta's mother. She died suddenly during the night."

To Anna's everlasting shame, her first reaction was one of relief that Todd was not leaving her for another woman, which was the first conclusion she had leapt to. And then she felt absolutely appalled with herself, remembering some of the unendurable pain of her own parents' death.

"Oh, Todd," she told him shakily. "I'm so very sorry. Poor Elisabeta. How is she?"

"She's okay," he said slowly. "Well, *fairly* okay. Her mother was a very old woman who had been sick for a long time. And whilst Elisabeta was kind of expecting this, knew that it was inevitable, perhaps was even for the best—well, it's still her mother, and people say that it's a terrible loss, no matter how expected." His voice softened. "But you know that, don't you, my darling?"

She heard the affection and the compassion in his voice for both her *and* Elisabeta, and even while she admired him for those qualities it only increased her feelings of vulnerability. Feelings which must be pretty strong if she had thought that he was about to *leave* her.

"So I suppose you'll be staying on?" she ventured.

"Well, yes. Until after the funeral. It's next week. But only if that's okay with you."

Well, what could she possibly say? He had already been gone for almost four weeks, which was longer than she had wanted, especially when there were so many unresolved issues between them. The child in her wanted to scream that, no, it *wasn't* okay. That he was her husband and she wanted him back where he should be. With her and their children, and not with Elisabeta.

But her selfish thoughts evaporated as she thought of Elisabeta, of how much she had sacrificed for her mother, and of the huge, gaping loss there must be in her life now.

Anna's voice softened with sympathy. "Of course it's okay, Todd," she whispered softly. "Take as long as you need."

"It shouldn't be any longer than that," he told her.

"The trip to Germany was a success and the weather is on course to provide the best harvest that they've had in years and years. In fact, if things all go according to plan, then the vineyard looks as though it's set to make a substantial profit within the next couple of years—for the first time in its history."

"Yes." He seemed so involved in Elisabeta's vineyard and Elisabeta's life that Anna had to remind herself that this was what Todd was like. His success was entirely due to his persistence and dedication. When he took something on, he took it on one hundred and ten per cent, which was why he had that elusive Midas touch which others in the City talked about so enviously. She forced herself to sound enthusiastic. "Well, that's marvellous, isn't it?" she said brightly. "And when the shock of losing her mother is less intense, then I expect that Elisabeta will think so, too."

"Oh, she does," he concurred softly. "She does. And how about you, darling?" he added, almost as an afterthought. "What have you been doing?"

Bearing in mind what Tina had said about disliking secrets, Anna opened her mouth to tell him what she had been up to, then thought better of it. She told herself that it was an inappropriate time to start banging on about how much weight she had lost, and how much she had grown to adore exercise, or that Russell thought that he could market her whole change of image in a glossy new book.

For wouldn't it be extremely insensitive to tell him things as frivolous as that, when he was in a house which was grieving?

And besides, wasn't there a part of her which wanted to surprise him? To dazzle him?

For years Anna hadn't given her appearance much thought beyond making sure that she was clean and presentable, but the episode in the restaurant had dented a huge hole in her confidence. The unkind comments of the two women who had been all over Todd had forced Anna to see herself as others saw her. As a very ordinary woman who was married to an extraordinary man. Well, that could spell the beginning of the end—everyone knew that.

Time after time she had seen articles in the newspapers about men who had outgrown their wives and traded them in for a younger, sexier model. And, whilst she did not imagine for a moment that Todd's morals were so shallow that *he* might do the same, nonetheless she was going to do her very best to keep temptation out of his way!

He had left the country and said goodbye to a plump frump of a wife.

Let him return to a streamlined version who might, just *might* also become a best-seller in the highly lucrative diet-book market!

Well, she could *dream*!

''Me?'' she queried disingenuously, and actually had the confidence to flash a secret smile at herself in the mirror which hung in the hall above the telephone. ''Oh, you know me, Todd. Nothing much.''

CHAPTER EIGHT

THE taxi screeched to a halt in front of the mansion building and Todd pulled three crisp notes from his wallet and handed them to the driver, who blinked with delight.

"Cor! That's very generous of you!" he exclaimed. "Thanks, Gov!"

"Thanks for getting me here," smiled Todd wryly, biting back his instinctive comment that he felt lucky to *be* back here! The taxi driver had clearly felt an affinity with the fastest of Formula One racing drivers, judging by the speed he had used on the journey back from Heathrow! Todd slammed the cab door behind him and stepped out into the early evening.

The dusk was curiously intense with the bright half-light so typical of spring, and he sighed with pleasure. He had missed England much more than he had thought, and his wife and family even more.

He noted the mass of daffodils which danced golden in window-boxes up and down the road, then raised his head to look at his own flat, since Anna could always be relied on to put on a magnificent display of spring flowers.

His grey eyes widened with surprise as he noted that there were *no* flowers this year. Not a daffodil or a tulip or even a grape hyacinth, which they both loved so much, and which Todd had often teased her were the exact colour of her eyes. Not one! How peculiar, he thought as he unlocked the heavy front door.

Deciding to give the ancient lift a miss, Todd took the stairs two by two, carrying his bulky suitcase and briefcase as lightly as if they had been empty, instead of packed to the brim with all kinds of presents for the girls and Anna!

He reached the door of their flat and contemplated knocking, then thought better of it. He wanted to surprise the girls, and to surprise his wife, too. He glanced at his watch and wondered what they might be doing.

Seven o'clock.

His memory focused with a poignant clarity as he acknowledged once again how much he had missed them.

They might be sitting doing their homework right now, with Anna helping them as she so often did, their four blonde heads bent over the maths which they all—apart from Tasha and her father—found so difficult.

Or they might still be finishing supper, sitting in a companionable mess among fruit cores and crumbs. Anna might even have made one of her delicious casseroles... Todd's mouth watered. He hoped so. The food on the plane had both looked *and* smelt disgusting and he had given it a very wide berth. And, whilst the food he had eaten while he was away had been delicious, there was nothing quite like *home* cooking.

He shut the front door quietly behind him and soundlessly put his suitcase and briefcase down on the carpet, then raised his eyebrows slightly. Instead of the usual sound of childish chatter, laughter and squabbling, he heard the deep throb of a double bass as an unfamiliar jazz record drifted down the corridor from the sitting room. And then he heard the sound of a laugh which was both familiar and strange and which made his heart instinctively stand still.

Anna's laugh.

Todd's dark brows met in a quizzical frown as he attempted to work out why her laughter sounded so strange, when he heard another laugh, only this time much deeper and more resonant.

A man's laugh.

So who was she entertaining? he wondered, attempting to keep mild irritation at bay, since he had wanted to find his family on their own. Which of their friends had come round to keep her company?

He moved silently along the corridor towards the vast sitting room, intrigued and more than a little disconcerted as he wondered what he would discover there and why he felt quite so uneasy. For surely to God he wasn't feeling *suspicious* of Anna? He had never had reason to distrust his wife, and never imagined a situation occurring where he would. She was simply not the kind of woman who would betray your trust.

But as he moved in front of the doorway Todd's heart picked up fast and furious speed as he stared at the scene which greeted him—Anna and Russell Goldsmith, halfway through what looked like a second bottle of very expensive champagne.

Anna was sprawled out full-length on one of the peacock-green sofas, with a denim-clad Russell sitting almost slavishly at her feet, though it actually took a moment or two for Todd to realise that it *was* Anna.

Because for a moment there he *didn't recognise his own wife*!

Anna chose just that moment to reach forward to touch Russell's cheek, and yet Todd was so stunned by her appearance that for a moment he found the intimate gesture far less threatening than Anna's brand-new look.

Dear Lord, he thought, with a sudden lurching of his heart. What had she done to herself?

For a start she looked skinny.

Well, not skinny exactly, but a good deal lighter than she had been when he had left. Whereas before her hips had looked resolutely child-bearing, now they just had an immensely feminine and flattering curve.

And she had clearly been working out, for there was fine muscular definition around her upper arms, and her abdomen looked much firmer. While her breasts, in comparison, seemed so much fuller as they strained against the fitted cornflower silk sweater she wore...a sweater he'd never seen before...teamed with a new pair of white jeans which made the high, pert swell of her bottom look very, very touchable.

But it was her hair which really threw him. Because the buttery, silken tresses in which for years he had feverishly buried his hands and his lips had been severely lopped off so that now they hung to her shoulders, the ends feathered to frame her face. And she had acquired a fringe, too, which seemed to draw attention to her kohl-ringed and mascaraed eyes, making them seem bluer and wider than ever before.

And guiltier too, he thought with sudden disdain as he looked deep into their azure depths and surprised the unfamiliar and unwelcome emotion there as her hand fell like a stone from Russell's cheek and she sat back, as if she'd been stung.

Yes, guilt, thought Todd grimly. He could almost smell it in the air. "Hello, Anna," he drawled.

Anna's reactions were slower than normal, but then normally she would not have drunk three glasses of champagne on an empty stomach before seven o'clock in the evening. She sat bolt upright, all the colour draining from her wine-flushed cheeks. "T-Todd," she stammered, sounding as conscience-stricken as a child caught with her hand in the cookie jar. "I w-wasn't expecting you."

"That much is obvious," came his disparaging agreement as Todd dampened down the greatest rage he had ever experienced and turned his steely grey eyes on Russell, who was now fast scrabbling to his feet.

"Hello, Todd!" Russell attempted a jolly tone which did not quite come off. "Nice to see you!"

Todd looked around the room, failing to return the superficial and meaningless platitude with one of his own. "Where's Saskia?" he enquired with cold interest.

A dull brick colour stained Russell's neck. "She's not here, actually."

"No. So I see. And just where *is* she?"

"She's—er—she's at home, actually."

"Oh." Todd's voice sent a shiver down Anna's spine and then he directed a look of icy anger at her, which made her even more uneasy. "How very convenient."

His disdain ignited a feeling of indignation in Anna. Yes, he had found her in what *looked* like a compromising position, but how about showing a little *trust* here? He had probably shared countless bottles of wine like this with Elisabeta, so what earthly right did he have to stand there like some dark, avenging angel? And with one of their mutual friends, too!

She met his accusing gaze head-on. ''Todd, I really don't think—''

''Where are the children?'' he demanded, cutting across her words without a qualm.

''There's a music concert at school.''

''Then why aren't you there, too?'' he snapped.

''Because...'' Anna looked at Russell helplessly, and that silent appeal for collusion stabbed at Todd's heart like a sabre blow.

''I think I'd better go.'' Russell avoided Todd's eye.

Anna shook her head. ''Please don't go,'' she implored, because she had never seen Todd look at her like this before, with that dangerous kind of anger hardening his features so that he didn't even *look* like her husband at the moment, but some brooding and implacable stranger. And surely if Russell stayed his presence would dilute that rage?

''I think you *had* better go, Russell.'' The words shot out of Todd's mouth like bullets, and Russell needed no second bidding.

Suddenly the laid-back casting director had all the composure of a cornered animal. He moved towards the door, knocking his empty champagne glass over in the process. ''Sure, sure,'' he babbled, his smooth, transatlantic drawl deserting him as he felt obliged to add conversationally, ''Good time in Romania, was it, Todd?''

Todd found that he was only *just* hanging onto his

temper and it took him a monumental effort to remember that Russell and Saskia had been friends of theirs for years.

But did that excuse Russell from fawning all over Anna the way he had been? Todd certainly wouldn't have put himself in such a compromising situation with *Russell's* wife, but there again he doubted whether Saskia would have invited him to.

Todd captured Russell's disingenuous look within his steely gaze and managed a grim glimmer of a smile for propriety's sake. "Romania was fine," he said succinctly. "But I haven't seen my wife or family in over a month, and I'd really like to talk to Anna alone, if you don't mind, Russell. Come on, I'll see you out."

He took an awfully long time to get back, and it was only when the repeated sound of doors being opened and closed imprinted itself on her subconscious that Anna realised he must have been peering into every room like a detective!

Enough was enough, she decided. She sat up properly as he walked back into the room, trying to ignore the muzzy feeling which was fogging her mind. "Have you just been searching the flat?" she wanted to know. "You weren't checking up on me, were you, Todd?"

He met the challenge in her eyes with an icy stare. "And if I was?"

Anna could feel her heart hammering in her chest, and when she spoke she wasn't surprised to hear that her voice sounded thin and tremulous. "Just wh-what were you expecting to find?"

"Who knows?" he answered, with a flippant shrug of his shoulders, realising that this discussion was now escalating into a full-scale row. And that he seemed both unwilling and unable to prevent it. "After all, I wasn't expecting to find you alone in the flat with Russell."

A muscle working frantically in his cheek was the only sign that he was keeping his emotions tightly under control, and for the first time Anna became aware that he had acquired a faint tan in the few weeks he had been away.

Strange how a tan could set him apart, could distance him.

She felt odd and displaced, as though the man standing in front of her was a stranger, instead of her husband of over ten years. "You can't just walk in here and start haranguing Russell—"

"And what *should* I have done?" he demanded coldly. "Stood back and allowed you to continue draping yourself all over him like some second-rate siren?" His eyes swept over her in a candid stare which said nothing about admiration and everything about accusation as he commented at last on her appearance. "Just what have you been doing to yourself, Anna?"

Anna's heart plummeted. So that bald, critical sentence was the culmination of all her weeks of hard work, was it? She had eaten enough lettuce to make every rabbit in the Southern Hemisphere green with envy; she had swum and jogged and puffed her way through aerobic classes. And all for what? So that her husband could stand there with that censorious look blazing from his grey eyes?

She swallowed down her disappointment. "Are you objecting to my appearance, Todd?"

"I'm wondering what could have possibly inspired such a radical change," he returned evenly. "Not Russell, by any chance?"

Anna stared at him in genuine confusion. *"Russell?* Why would it have anything to do with Russell?"

"Well, he's here for a start. And on his own. Think about it. Doesn't a woman in the first throes of a love affair lose interest in everything other than the object of her desire?" he drawled. "Including food?"

"You think I've starved myself because I've been having an affair with Russell?" She almost laughed at the absurdity of the suggestion, but something in his face stopped her. "You can't be serious!"

"Can't I?" He turned away, and Anna honestly thought that he was about to walk right out of the apartment, until she realised that he was simply going to the drinks cabinet to pour himself a hefty shot of whisky—something he normally only did when they'd received bad news. When he turned back his face was dark, with a forbidding look which was quite alien to her; in all the years they had been married she had never seen him look quite like that before.

He sipped his drink and then put the glass on the mantelpiece. "There's no need to sound so outraged, Anna," he told her unblinkingly. "What am I supposed to think? I walk in unexpectedly to find you half-cut—"

"I am *not* half-cut!" she declared indignantly, then spoilt it all by hiccuping. "Okay, I admit—I had a few glasses of champagne—"

"A few? You were lying sprawled with abandon, stroking Russell's cheek!" he accused.

"I was not *s-stroking* Russell's cheek!" she spluttered. "I happened to be removing a speck of dust from the side of his mouth!"

"Really?" He elevated his dark eyebrows in a look of mocking disdain. "Then it's a good thing he didn't have dust on any other parts of his anatomy, isn't it? Or were you just getting started?"

"Don't be so crude!" she snapped.

"Why not?" he sneered. "I thought that's what you liked! You certainly demonstrated your approval of crudity during a couple of fairly spectacular incidents just before I left for Romania, didn't you, Anna?"

She almost blushed as he alluded to that unforgettable episode of lovemaking on his office desk, but the mention of Romania allowed a little sanity to seep back into her befuddled brain. *He* had swanned off for a month, hadn't he? So was she just going to take all these unfounded insults squarely on the nose?

Like *hell* she was!

"What gives you the right to come marching in here, to jump to a whole heap of thoroughly unreasonable conclusions and then to start cataloguing them?" Anna stormed. "After all, I'm not so naive as to think you didn't share a bottle of wine with Elisabeta during your *four-week sortie*," she added deliberately.

"That's different," he said stubbornly.

"How is it different?" she challenged.

"I've known Elisabeta—"

"And if you come out with all that old twaddle about Elisabeta being like a sister to you I think I'll scream!" Anna declared passionately. "It all boils down to trust, surely? Either you think I want an affair with Russell or you don't! And to imply that my lib-

erated sexual behaviour with you before you went
away has somehow turned me into some kind of in-
satiable nymphomaniac is nothing short of *insulting*,
Todd Travers!''

He took another mouthful of whisky and grimaced,
the intelligent and reasoning side of his nature ac-
knowledging the truth which lay behind her words. So
why this unfamiliar and elemental streak which had
sneakily emerged and which was stubbornly refusing
to listen to reason? ''You've lost a lot of weight,'' he
observed slowly.

Anna could have wept.

The weight she had lost was somehow incidental.
She had done it mostly to prove that she *could* do it.
To show a society which equated fatness with failure
that she *wasn't* a failure. The achievement had been
more in the process itself than in the end result. And
yes, she *was* slimmer, but not excessively so—she had
merely got rid of the excess weight which had lingered
on far too long after her daughters had been born.
Much more importantly she *felt* better. And she was
fitter and healthier, too. ''Oh! So you noticed!'' she
quipped sarcastically.

''Of course I noticed!'' he drawled, and paused very
deliberately. ''And you've had your hair cut, too.''

''Yes.'' She met the look in his eyes and the words
came tumbling out of her mouth, even though she de-
spised herself for needing his approval quite so much.
''And...do you like it?''

''I liked it before,'' he told her oddly.

Her mouth threatened to pucker. ''So is that a yes,
Todd? Or a no?''

He *should* have told her that he had loved her hair

when he could pick up great silken handfuls of it, but his comments continued to clip out as if they were in the middle of a particularly difficult business negotiation. "Why did you have to change it?"

Anna opened her eyes very wide. "But I thought that you were the great advocate of change!" she told him triumphantly. "And when I voiced doubt about change for the sake of it you poured scorn all over my reservations!"

"That's different!" he snapped.

"*How* is it different?" she howled. "*You* were the one who said that we were in a rut. Those were *your* words, Todd, not mine! You were the one who set the ball rolling, and maybe I just came round to your way of thinking. I took a good, long look at myself after you'd gone away, and I didn't like what I saw. In fact, I didn't like it one bit! I was living in a time-warp!"

"What do you mean by a time-warp?"

"I mean that I was still the same girl you met in that nightclub all those years ago! Or rather I *looked* the same! Same old Anna with the same old hairstyle and the same old make-up! The only thing which was different about me was that I'd added six kilos to my hips and bottom!"

"But I didn't *care* about that," he told her softly.

"And neither did I," came her candid reply. "Until you invited me out for lunch that day—"

"Oh, for heaven's *sake*!" he objected, briefly closing his eyes as he anticipated what she was about to say. "How can a woman of your intelligence allow the bitchy comments of two desperate and jealous women to affect you?"

"But what we're talking about has absolutely nothing to do with intelligence, Todd—we're talking gut reaction here! And they were right! In fact, they did me a favour! I *did* look an absolute fright—and nothing like the sort of woman that most people would expect a man like you to be married to!''

''Anna—''

''No!'' She shook her newly styled head firmly but her hair no longer swung in disarray down her back. ''Please let me have my say! I was just sweet Anna. Docile Anna. The little nurturing and caring wife at home. The big *mama* standing over the cooking pot. Even you commented on it. You began to talk about what would happen when the girls got older and began to get more and more independent, and I found myself asking the same question. And I got *frightened,* Todd!''

This new, slim and beautiful Anna was like a stranger to him, but even so fear was the last emotion he would have associated with his wife. He remembered how she had given birth to three babies when she was still in her teens herself, an experience which would have bamboozled many other, older women. But not Anna. She had borne the pain of her labour with nothing but trust and pride. Todd narrowed his eyes with surprise. ''You? Frightened?''

''Yes, frightened! Is that so very alien to you, Todd? You have your career—you'll always have your career—''

''Not necessarily.''

''Oh, come on, Todd,'' she sighed. ''Don't forget this is *me* you're talking to. And I know you! I know how you operate! You have a need to succeed which has absolutely nothing to do with money. You earned enough money for us to live on comfortably for the rest of our lives a long, long time ago, didn't you? But it was never enough. It never *will* be enough. Whatever happens in our life, Todd, you will continue to go out and work, because that's the way you're made. Success gives you the kind of buzz that nothing else can. And I thought—well, where does that leave *me*?''

She took a deep breath. ''When the girls have gone off to university, or are mucking out stables or treading the boards or whatever path in life they choose, well, what does Anna do then? Particularly if she's holed up in some god-forsaken mud-bath in the country, which is what *you* seem to want to do.''

He shook his head, his voice gentle. ''We don't *have* to move to the country, you know, not if you've set your heart against it.''

But Anna shook her head. ''Oh, no! I can't oppose what I know would be a life-enhancing move for everyone—probably even me if I'm being perfectly honest—just because I don't like change. I'm happy to give it a try—but please don't raise any objections if I start to instigate a few modifications in my *own* life.''

Todd smiled. ''So *that's* what the weight loss is all about, is it? Just a change of image?''

Something in the comfortable and relaxed way he said it filled Anna with both anger and dread. She was so mad she could barely get the words out. ''How… how *dare* you *patronise* me by dismissing it all so lightly! This isn't *just* about anything, Todd!''

Todd crossed his arms over his chest, put his head to one side and studied her for a long moment, before he nodded, as if he had just come to a decision. "Point taken. And I think we've played this home-coming all wrong, don't you, sweetheart? I think we should start from the beginning and that I should come over there and do what I should have done—"

"If you hadn't found me in such an 'intimate' and 'compromising' position with Russell?" she put in sweetly.

His mouth hardened. Why bring that up now? "Let's leave that *particular* topic, shall we, Anna?" he grated. "Though just before we do I'd like to say that *your* motives may have been entirely blame-less—" he remembered her guilty look, but firmly pushed the thought away "—but I suspect that Russell's agenda may be different."

"Because?"

A dark, possessive light flared in Todd's eyes "Well, for a start, he's a *man*."

"With his brain located somewhere in his trousers, I suppose?"

"*Anna!*" Todd protested, and Anna might have gig-gled at the shocked expression on his face if the sub-ject hadn't been so deadly serious. "Where on earth did you hear an expression like that?"

"In the real world," said Anna grimly. "The world which I've been hidden away from all my adult life!"

Todd's eyes were suddenly sharp, all irrational thoughts of Russell obliterated by the knowledge of what lay behind his wife's distress. "And what else did you learn, Anna?" he asked quietly.

This was her moment, her moment of true indepen-dence, and she was going to relish every single second of it. Her smile was serene, her voice soft. "Oh, I think you'd be amazed at the different things I've learnt over the last few weeks, Todd.''

Grey eyes hardened into suspicious silver chips. ''What kind of things?''

She giggled as she interpreted his wariness, light-headed with the potential impact of her news. ''Not the kind that you're obviously thinking of, if you're about to get all suspicious again!'' she chided. She drew a deep breath. ''You see, Saskia has been photographing my weight loss and exercise programme over the last few weeks, and I've been liaising with Premium's nutrition department...''

''Is this some sort of riddle?'' Todd frowned.

''And the result of all this hard work will be out on the shelves in the next couple of weeks!'' she breezed on, as if he hadn't spoken.

''Would you mind telling me what you're talking about, Mrs Travers?''

She smiled, her eyes shiny with nerves and excitement. ''Of course I don't mind, darling! I'm talking about the latest diet book to hit the shelves—that's what I'm talking about.''

''Diet book?'' he echoed slowly.

''Uh-huh. It's called *Premium Wand—The Magic Way to Lose Weight, with Anna Travers.*'' Seeing that he still looked utterly bemused, she decided to enlighten him. ''You were the one who suggested that I needed a career—well, now I've got one! Don't you understand what I'm saying? I've written a book, Todd! I'm going to be famous!''

CHAPTER NINE

THERE was a moment of stunned silence before Todd said in an oddly rough and gritty voice, "I think you'd better start explaining, Anna."

It was the only negative reaction she had received since beginning the project, and Anna felt the first faint stirrings of misgiving. "It was Saskia's idea," she babbled nervously. "She thought that women who wanted to lose weight could identify with me—being an ordinary sort of mum, and all that. Well," she amended hastily as she saw the expression of disbelief which had hardened his features. "As ordinary as you *can* be when you've got a millionaire husband!"

She cleared her throat even more nervously. "I think what they meant was ordinary-*looking*! Anyway, Premium Stores were very keen on the idea. Saskia took the photos, and I came up with some of my recipes and we basically halved the fat content, and substituted yoghurt for cream—the usual sort of thing—you know? And the proofs look fantastic, Todd—just wait till you see them!" She searched his features anxiously for some sort of pleased reaction, but that obdurate expression was not what she'd been hoping for.

And when he still said nothing she raced on. "That's why Russell was here tonight, and why we were drinking champagne to celebrate. He brought the proofs round, you see.''

''Yes, I think I do,'' he said slowly, his expression still giving away nothing but displeasure. ''And the girls? What have the girls been doing while you were off being pampered and having your photographs taken?''

The anger which had been simmering away since he had walked in on her and started jumping to all the wrong conclusions finally boiled over. ''What do you *think* they were doing?'' she challenged.

''I don't know, do I? That's why I'm asking.''

''They were either at school or I asked Mrs Hobbs, the babysitter, to look after them—but that's beside the point, Todd.''

''I don't think so.''

''Well, let me change your mind for you—you arrogant man! I have spent the last ten years caring for our children to the best of my ability. I've always been there for them when they needed me and I think that I'm the best person to judge when and *if* they need me! If any of them had been ill or upset then I would have cancelled the job, but they weren't. They were pleased for me! And you can't have it both ways, Todd! You can't try and coax me away from devoting all my time to the triplets, and then berate me when I do!''

''Then why all the bloody *secrecy*?'' he exploded. ''Why the hell didn't you tell me you were writing a book?''

''Because I wanted it to be a surprise! I wanted you to come back to a new-look wife—it was supposed to give you *pleasure*! And don't act so hard done by just because I didn't tell you about it—you certainly didn't give me a complete breakdown of every second you spent in *Elisabeta's* company, did you?''

They stood surveying each other across the sitting room, the few feet separating them seeming to Anna like an unbreachable gulf. She had ached for him and longed for him for weeks, and yet now this great chasm lay between them.

Why, Todd had not touched her since he had first entered the room. Nor even kissed her. She stared at his lips and her mouth trembled violently as desire and resentment fused.

Todd saw the shivering of her lips and that one simple gesture set his pulses racing, fueling his own desire; it took only seconds for that desire to reach a rapid and almost unbearably heated pitch.

Even from where she stood Anna could observe the sudden darkening of his eyes and she felt her blood thicken in response, felt the thrilling little pulses as her breasts tingled into life, even though a part of her despaired of her instantaneous response to him. Because she didn't want to make love with him. Not now. Not yet—when there was so much between them which had not been said.

''Anna,'' he began, in a throaty murmur, when the clanging of the doorbell had the effect of a bucket of ice water being poured over the pair of them.

Anna swallowed, trying to disassociate herself from the remorseless aching he had provoked. ''That'll be the girls,'' she managed through dry lips which did not seem to function properly.

''I'll go,'' he told her grittily, and hesitated for a moment as their gazes merged and Anna found herself waiting breathlessly for some kind of reparation. But a small shake of his dark head indicated his reluctance to say anything more, and, with shoulders set in tension, he went off to greet his daughters.

And Anna was left to watch his retreating form in silence, wondering why her whole world should suddenly feel as though it was falling around her.

At least the exuberant delight with which the triplets greeted their father meant that an atmosphere between Todd and Anna was impossible to maintain, and both of them endeavoured to appear as normal as possible—but it wasn't easy, not after weeks of separation.

Anna drank black coffee and cooked a heap of eggs and bacon while the girls excitedly unwrapped the gifts he had brought back with him.

Of the three girls, only Tasha seemed to sense that something was not quite right between her mother and father and she screwed up her freckle-dusted nose the way she always did when she was worried.

"Is something wrong, Mummy?" she asked, her blue eyes narrowed with question as she watched her mother melt the butter in the frying pan.

Anna's stomach clenched with fear as she dropped an egg into the pan. She had preached honesty as a policy since their daughters were knee-high to a grasshopper, so how could she fudge a question like that? But surely it would only frighten them if she told them the truth—that, yes, things weren't right between Mummy and Daddy, and she wasn't sure how she could make them right again. "Why do you ask?" she prevaricated brightly, sliding the egg onto Tasha's plate.

Tasha shrugged, and immediately stabbed at the

yolk with a toast soldier, so that it seeped a sticky yellow puddle all over her plate. "Because you aren't eating anything. And you look awfully pale."

"I'm not feeling too good," answered Anna, pleased at least to be able to make *this* observation a truthful one.

"Mummy drank a little too much champagne with Uncle Russell," put in Todd, his eyes glittering with mockery. "Didn't you, darling?"

"Uncle Russell spends *loads* of time round here!" piped up Tina.

"Oh, does he?" asked Todd softly.

"He's been liaising with me about the book!" Anna was aware that her voice sounded shrill and defensive, but how dared Todd involve the girls in his totally irrational jealousy?

"Mummy's book comes out next month," observed Tally excitedly.

"So she tells me," said Todd.

"Aren't you pleased, Daddy?" queried Tasha. "That Mummy's going to be rich and famous?"

"Of course I'm pleased," answered Todd carefully.

"And she says I can wear jodhpurs to the launch!" babbled Tally. "She's going to buy me a pair!"

Todd met Anna's eyes over three blonde, curly heads. "Oh? Just for the launch?"

Anna had meant *this* to be a surprise, too, but as her surprises seemed to have a habit of failing spectacularly she decided to tell him now. "No, not just for the launch. I thought it would be best to have a pair for when she gets her new horse!"

"Because Mummy says she *will* go and live in the country!" declared Tally, hugging her arms across her chest, as if her mother's agreement was the most precious gift in the world. "She told us while you were staying with Aunty Elisabeta."

"That's wonderful," said Todd quietly, and the soft silver glance he sent blazing towards her made Anna's heart beat out a rapid tattoo.

But she was determined that her face should give nothing away, for she was still angry with him. He had made all kinds of unsavoury accusations about her behaviour with Russell, so did he just think that she would forget all about them? Pretend they'd never been said?

It wasn't until the girls had gone to bed and fallen asleep that Anna and Todd were finally alone again, and they eyed each other warily.

"Let's go to bed," he said suddenly, his voice roughened by an urgent need to be close to her.

She wanted to hurt him, as he had hurt her with his accusatory words, but her own desire was far too strong to inflict the only effective punishment she could think of. Because he would have needed to have done something very bad indeed for Anna not to have melted into his arms after four and a half arid weeks without him...

She was strangely shy as she undressed, aware that he was watching her in a new way. And suddenly she found herself longing for her old body back—the plumper, more comfortable version she had worked so hard to rid herself of. For at least that old, familiar Anna had felt in control, had known what to expect from her relationship with Todd.

Or had she?

Whereas now it was like the first time all over again,

only without that wild impetuosity of youthful love. And Todd was watching her with an intensity which filled her with trepidation as well as anticipation.

"Don't be shy," he whispered as he saw her fingers falter, then hesitate by the clasp of her bra.

She met his eyes, her cheeks growing pink as she let it flutter to the floor. "I don't think I'm cut out for stripping!" she joked.

"On the contrary," he murmured huskily. "You were absolutely made for it!"

He watched each garment as it was removed from her body, feeling more than a little voyeuristic as he did so, and yet curiously reluctant to help her. It was a new Anna who stood before him, removing frivolous pieces of filmy underwear which were half familiar, and he realised that she was wearing some of the lingerie he had brought back from his various trips abroad. He had often wondered vaguely in the past why she had not worn them, but now he understood perfectly. For these tiny scraps of nonsense could not be worn by a woman who had robust curves.

"You look wonderful," he told her truthfully.

"It's beautiful underwear," she prevaricated.

He shook his head. "That isn't what I meant, Anna. You don't need to gild your body with silk and lace to look wonderful." His hands were trembling as he took her into his arms, kissing her deeply for the first time since he had arrived home, and it was like the sweetest rain falling on parched and unforgiving ground, for he drank her in as though he couldn't get enough of her.

She was dazed by the time he lifted his head, and her eyes were dazzling blue stars.

"Oh, Todd," she whispered brokenly, aware that tears were not so very far away, and she found herself wishing that they could go back to a time when everything in their world seemed comfortable and predictable. Anna felt as though she was on a runaway train—hurtling to an unknown destination and not knowing what fate had in store for her there.

"Shh." He soothed her with his lips, anointing her cheeks and her eyebrows with tiny kisses, the tip of his tongue snaking a moist and erotic path all the way down her long neck to where the tips of her milky pale breasts fell willingly into his mouth. "It's okay, Anna, darling." He slid his hand between her thighs and she shuddered violently with pleasure. "Everything's going to be okay."

She swayed in his arms and let him carry her over to the large bed. He had seduced her in that very bed—the same bed in which she had grown heavy with the triplets, and where she had suckled them after their births, to the astonishment and delight of the medical team in charge of her care.

He pulled the duvet over her and took her wordlessly into his arms to kiss her again, and he discovered that touching this new Anna was intensely stimulating. His fingertips encountered unfamiliar indentations and hollows and the normally warm cushion of her belly was now iron-hard and flat. She *felt* completely different. She was Anna, and yet not Anna, and Todd found the sensations completely intoxicating.

It had been so long, he thought, with a strangled moan, as he thrust into her at last. And then, with a considerable effort, he put his own desire completely out of his mind until he had Anna exactly where he wanted her, sobbing out her fulfilment beneath him.

Afterwards he turned to look at her, lying soft-mouthed and smiling, her eyelashes two shadowed half-moons which brushed against her flushed cheeks.

"Asleep?" he whispered.

She opened her eyes immediately, her dreamy, satiated smile remaining firmly in place. "No."

He captured a shorter lock of butter-silk hair than he was used to, and twisted it experimentally around his finger.

"Do you like my hair?" she asked. "Really?"

"You mean after my appallingly negative response when I first saw it?" His mouth twisted self-deprecatingly. "Anna, you look magnificent. Modern, sleek, young and beautiful—and nothing like the mother of ten-year-old triplets!" He frowned as he finished his observation, suddenly aware that apprehension was slowly tiptoeing its way up his naked spine. Because Anna had transformed herself into the kind of woman who would bring out the predator in most men. He felt the unfamiliar lurch of jealousy as it twisted like a knife in his stomach.

"Thank you," she murmured, but couldn't miss the unmistakable darkening of his face.

He forced himself to show an interest in her book. "So when's the launch of this wonder book?"

"In two weeks' time."

"That seems very quick," he commented, and sent her a quirky smile. "From what little I know about publishing!"

"It *is* very quick," agreed Anna. "Mainly because Premium are backing the whole scheme and the girls are household names. The launch will coincide with the triplets' announcement that they're giving up modelling and that there's a hunt on for their successors! That's why they didn't want to hang around.''

"I see," said Todd slowly.

"Plus they're planning to stock the book in every one of their retail outlets, as well as bookstores, so sales are looking very hopeful.'' She let her eyelids flutter sleepily down once more.

"Wow!'' Todd expelled a long, slow breath from between his lips and his eyes were rueful as he stared down at his wife. "And that's how the triplets want to play it, is it? A wham-bam finish instead of a gradual easing out?''

"Yes," she told him firmly. "And if that's what they've made their minds up to do, then what is the point of prolonging it?''

"None at all, I guess.''

"We can even start looking at places to live—in the country. So you'd better find some for us to view!'' she finished, with a smile which cost her more than she knew—and Todd noticed.

He felt his heart thunder as he acknowledged the sweet generosity of her gesture, the loving smile which had softened her features so that, for all her weight loss and change of image, she actually looked exactly like the young woman who had first ensnared him in the nightclub.

Todd was instantly smitten by his conscience. "You know, we don't have to—''

But she shook her head so that her hair tangled in a silken mesh all over the pillow. "Oh, yes, we do. I want to give it a try, Todd," she told him firmly. "The best try I can. For the girls' sakes, and for all our sakes.''

And now he owed her something, too. A gesture he was oddly reluctant to make, and yet knew he *had* to make, in fairness to his wife. ''I had no right to make those accusations concerning you and Russell, sweetheart.''

She snuggled up to him, growing slumberous now with the blissful aftermath of great sex, and the resolution of where they might live. ''That's okay,'' she said easily. ''I guess you walked into a situation that might easily have been misconstrued.''

''But I had no right to say some of the things I said,'' he repeated quietly. ''Especially when our relationship has been based on trust. And suspicion erodes trust.'' He tenderly kissed her forehead. ''It was wrong of me to suspect Russell,'' he added reluctantly, even though the words tasted bitter on his tongue. But say it he must. Todd had seen enough of life to know the highly destructive nature of unfounded jealousy. And he certainly shouldn't feel jealous of a man they had both known as a friend for years. ''Forgive me?'' he whispered.

''Mmm, you know I do. Silly, gorgeous man,'' sighed Anna, nestling contentedly into the crook of his arm and just about to fall asleep when she realised there was one question that she had omitted to ask him. ''And how's Elisabeta?''

''Elisabeta?'' he echoed.

''Mmm. You didn't say very much.''

She felt rather than saw him smile through a voice which was now slurred with the combined fatigue of air travel and spent passion. ''Oh, Elisabeta's fine.''

It told her precisely nothing, but Todd had—quite rightly—said that suspicion eroded trust.

And just before she herself drifted off to sleep Anna made a silent vow that she, too, would be distrustful no more...

CHAPTER TEN

WITH a fortnight to go, and counting, the launch of Anna's new book took precedence over everything else in the Travers family home. And the fact that the launch coincided with the triplets' bowing out of public life clearly caught the imagination of the general public.

The telephone in the flat began ringing first thing every morning, and went on ringing so often during the day and beyond that Todd had taken to leaving it off the hook, in order to eat an uninterrupted supper with his family.

"That's all anyone ever wants to talk about these days," complained Tasha over breakfast one morning. "Mummy's new diet book! I'm sick of hearing about it!"

Anna looked up from where she was scraping off half the marmalade she had absently and very liberally smothered all over her piece of toast. She was fast discovering that *becoming* a sylphlike version of her former self was not the problem, it was having the will-power to *stay* that way! She was thinking of bringing out a sequel to her diet book entitled *Staying Slim is Hard Work!* But, of course, nobody would ever dare to publish *that* because it was much too close to the truth!

"That isn't terribly fair, Tasha, darling," Anna commented mildly. "The press are terribly interested in the fact that you girls are giving up your Premium job at last—you know they are!"

"More interested in finding our replacement, you mean!" Tally reflected rather dramatically.

Anna resisted the urge to point out that it was all very well for the girls to start grumbling about being replaced—*they* had been the ones who had been so keen to leave to pursue other interests!

The post dealt with, Anna flicked her way through a glossy clutch of brochures advertising house details, just in time to see Todd enter the kitchen at speed, while deftly knotting a tie of topaz silk. He looked tired, she thought. Very tired. With blue smudges shadowing his heavily lashed grey eyes.

Mind you, perhaps it wasn't really surprising that he was tired, because in the two weeks since he had been back they had been rediscovering each other, especially in a physical sense. Sex seemed to be at the top of both their agendas, in a way it had not been for years. At night, they could hardly wait for the triplets to go to bed before the two of them would creep into their bedroom and fall into bed themselves, giggling with guilt and pleasure at the thought of the night to come.

Along with her weight, Anna had also shed a lot of her shyness. Quite often now she made the first move in bed, and the obvious pleasure that it gave Todd only increased her confidence to try things she would never have dared to try before. Once or twice she had caught him sending her a narrow-eyed glance as he moved helplessly beneath her.

"Where did you learn to do *that*?" he would gasp.

"From my imagination," would come her smug reply.

But Anna also guessed that he was having a little trouble adjusting to her new-found lack of inhibition, her willingness to take the lead where before it had usually been Todd who had taken the sexual initiative.

Consequently, sleep had been at a premium.

Todd kissed and ruffled the top of each blonde, curly head as he said good morning to his daughters. "Go and get ready for school," he instructed them. "And I'll drop you off, if you're lucky!"

Amidst excited squeals, the triplets exited the kitchen and Todd sat down at the table, poured himself a strong black coffee, then picked up a piece of buttered toast and bit into it hungrily. "My appetite seems to be *huge* just lately," he commented, with a sardonic drawl. "I can't *imagine* why!"

Anna looked up at him hopefully, trying to gauge his mood. "Do you happen to be free on Friday afternoon?" she asked.

He stared across the table at her, remembering just what the minxy woman had been up to less than an hour ago. The memory of it made him want to drag her off somewhere where they could be alone again, but memories like that made him hot under the collar and were not conducive to a full day's work, so he pushed them firmly to the back of his mind and loosened his tie instead. "Why?"

Anna sighed. She knew he wasn't going to like what she had to say, but *he* wasn't the one being pressurised by the publishers. "The *Daily View* want to do a big interview with me to tie in with the book launch," she began. "And they want the girls, too," she added, fixing him with an optimistic look.

"So?"

Goodness, he *was* in a bad mood, thought Anna. That was the last time she was going to wake him up at six in the morning to anoint him with kisses! "So they'd like you to be in it, too! The whole Travers family."

Todd shook his head and shuddered. "Sorry, Anna—no can do!"

"But *Todd*!" she beseeched him. "Think of all the publicity!"

"I *have* thought about it," he told her from between gritted teeth as his erotic memories of earlier became just that. "In fact, I've thought of very little else since I've been home. You seem to have been featured in some form or other—in about half the magazines down at the local news-stand! Not to mention that picture of you wearing a leotard on the back of our branflakes box!"

"Don't you like the picture?" she asked him anxiously as she turned round the packet in question, to peer at the still unexpected sight of a beaming Anna wearing a shiny turquoise leotard, with a bowl of branflakes in one hand and a copy of her book in the other!

He attempted to damp down his unreasonable annoyance. "It's a very good photo, Anna," he told her carefully. "But then *all* the photos in the book are good."

"I know," she said proudly. "Saskia and Russell are *terribly* pleased with them!"

"I'm so very glad!" he quipped sarcastically.

Anna frowned. "But you're not happy about something?"

Todd put his cup down. "Well, call me old-fashioned if you like, but I can't say that I find it particularly *easy* to conjure up much enthusiasm for the whole project…"

Anna crashed her cup down onto the saucer with disappointment. Just when they had been getting along so beautifully, too! Now he was about to come out with some negative comment which would probably spoil all her enjoyment! "Oh?" she questioned stonily. "And why's that?"

He scrutinised her very hard for a moment, then shook his head. "I don't think you want to hear."

"Oh, but that's where you're wrong, Todd. I do!"

Todd's mouth hardened. "Well, for a start, I'm not mad about the idea of you appearing on over one hundred pages wearing little more than a G-string and a pair of Lycra tights!"

Anna sucked in an indignant breath. "Oh, for goodness' sake! Women wear those kinds of outfits to fitness classes all over the world! They show less than you'd see on most beaches, so *please* don't be so ludicrous, Todd!"

He sighed. "I didn't say that my objections were rational, Anna—I'm just telling you how I feel, since you asked. And, if you must know, I'm fed up with journalists ringing up my secretary to find out what it's like being married to the new slimming icon! I was also," he continued remorselessly, "not very happy to see one of our wedding photos featured on page seven of *Slimmers Weekly*."

"I didn't want to give them *that*," she told him

miserably. "But they went on and on about it so much that in the end I just gave in."

Todd's jaw clenched. "Anna, I think it's wonderful that you've found a new interest—"

"Don't you *dare* patronise me!"

"I am *not* patronising you," he retorted, his voice growing cold. "I am merely pointing out that this new career of yours has the potential to grow into an unsightly and unmanageable beast if you let it. And it's up to you not to let it. That's all."

Oh, that was *all*, was it? thought Anna indignantly as she got up from the table and began to slam the dirty cups and plates into the dishwasher.

She felt his hands on her shoulders, but refused to turn round, even when he bent down to say softly, "Any chance we could get away to look at some of those houses this weekend?"

Part of her wanted to lean back into the warm security of his hard body, while the other railed against what she saw as Todd being restrictive. He had wanted her to have a career but then didn't seem to like it when she found one!

"I'll see what I can do," she said stiffly. "But I have to be fitted for the dress I'm wearing to the launch." She turned round then, screwing her face up anxiously. "You *will* be coming to the launch, won't you, Todd?"

He was feeling tired and bad-tempered. He stared at his wife, wondering what on earth had happened to her priorities. He had sat back and been as patient as he could be, but Anna hadn't looked at a single house since he'd been home. What was more, she showed no interest or desire to do so, either. He had tried telling himself that things would be different after the launch, but his patience was now wearing thin.

He had seen the enthusiasm with which the normally cynical publishing world had greeted his wife's collaboration with Saskia, Russell and Premium Stores. Todd wasn't stupid—he could see that Anna and her weight loss could run and run. Anyone with a modicum of business acumen could predict that there was huge earning potential in any books following on from *Premium Wand*. The question was, could the family bear the strain?

"You *will* be coming to the launch, Todd?" Anna repeated.

His eyes glittered. "I don't know, Anna. I haven't made up my mind yet."

Todd *did* attend the launch, which turned out to be a noisy, booze-fuelled scrum held in a sumptuous, chandelier-lit banqueting room in a large hotel in Marylebone. Unfortunately, he insisted on scowling every time a photographer had the temerity to point a lens in his direction and left long before everyone else, taking the triplets with him. They were most disgruntled to meet a cheeky little eight-year-old redhead, who was to be their replacement.

"She's *far* too young!" they had scoffed in unison.

"I'd better get these three home. I'll see you later," Todd had whispered in Anna's ear on the way out.

"You might!" she'd snapped back, then had hastily rearranged her face into a smile as she saw Russell shooting her a keen glance from across the other side of the room, and raising his glass of champagne to her.

But, despite her smile, Anna was furious.

Furious with Todd for going so early, *and* for taking the girls with him. Furious with herself for feeling bored and irritated by the whole bun fight. And furious with whoever had decided, in their infinite wisdom, to provide ''low-calorie' canapés. There was no food of any substance to blot up the copious amounts of champagne supplied by the publishers, and most of the journalists seemed barely able to pick a pen up, let alone write any copy!

Anna was dressed in a shiny silver mini-dress made out of what looked like chain-mail, which had been cleverly designed to show off her newly streamlined body. Of course, the push-up bra and constricting Lycra tights helped make the most of her new figure, while the rhinestone and silver earrings which dangled from her lobes like miniature chandeliers certainly gave her a *glittery* appearance. But Anna couldn't remember feeling this miserable for ages.

She had seen the book launch as a high point in her life, a further sign of her growing independence, but it all meant surprisingly little without her husband and children there to share it with her, she realised.

Why couldn't Todd just have hung around and waited for her, instead of escaping with the speed of a hamster whose cage door had been left open?

She pushed past a photographer and made her way out to the loo. In a minute she would announce that she was going home.

It had all been such a rush getting here this evening—chivvying the triplets to get changed, trying to keep Todd in a good mood so he wouldn't turn up with a thunderous expression. Though she might as well not have bothered because, judging by the grim, dark look on his face, he had clearly found the whole event a trial and an ordeal.

She stared hard into the mirror, barely recognising herself. She had submitted to a professional make-up job, which had left her feeling as though she would need to use a trowel to get a tenth of the gunge off. But, whatever the make-up artist had done to her, she had certainly effected a dramatic change in Anna's normally scrubbed and natural appearance.

Her face was pale, almost white, with two spots of colour along her cheekbones, which gave her a sort of wild, feverish look. Silver glittered on the lids of her blue eyes, which had been ringed by some dark and dramatic cobalt pencil. Consequently, Anna's eyes looked huge. And troubled, she thought, wishing she'd eaten before she had come out. She felt slightly nauseated, but then champagne on an empty stomach was a disastrous combination, and she was old enough to know that.

Anna stifled a yawn. Her face ached from smiling through so many inane photo poses, and her family had stomped off without her. All she wanted to do was to go home and kick these monstrous silver platform shoes off, but, as the "star" of the whole venture, she could hardly slip away unnoticed. Was this what she really wanted out of life? she found herself wondering.

She had just finished telling the head of Gordon Books, the publishers, that she was planning to leave shortly, when she felt a tap on her elbow, and she turned to find Russell standing there, an odd sort of smile on his mouth, his eyebrows raised in question.

"Not going, are you, beautiful?"

Even the way Russell was looking at her irritated her intensely. Anna couldn't remember ever feeling so niggly in all her life. "I am," she nodded. "They've got all the photos they need." She cast a disparaging eye around the room where the over-familiar body language between complete strangers bore testimony to the amount of champagne which had been consumed. "And things look as though they're degenerating around here. Everyone's *drunk*!"

Russell hastily slid his empty glass onto a passing waitress's tray. "Shall I call you a taxi, then?" he asked casually.

"I think there's a car provided," said Anna.

"Then mind if I tag along? The car can drop me off afterwards." He patted the back pocket of his trousers and gave a rueful shrug. "I brought my own motor, but I think I'm over the limit."

Anna tried to imagine Todd doing the same, but simply couldn't. His control was formidable. If he had planned to drive, then he would have stuck religiously to mineral water. How could a man be so reliable, thought Anna longingly, and yet also be so exciting and intriguing? He was the person she would most like to be marooned on a desert island with. How lucky she was, she thought happily, to be married to him!

"You don't mind giving me a lift, do you, Anna?" Russell frowned.

Anna smiled. "Of course I don't mind." Suddenly she couldn't wait to be home—home where she belonged, with her three gorgeous children and her gorgeous husband. And later…much later…locked tightly in Todd's arms… Anna shivered with anticipation.

"But I'd like to go right now, if you don't mind."
Her eyes searched the room. "Is Saskia ready?"

Russell looked evasive. "Oh, she isn't here. She
went on ahead. Charlie's babysitter couldn't stay for
the whole evening, so Saskia's gone to relieve her."

"Oh." Anna tried to shake off a vague feeling of
unease. "I see."

"The car will be out front," said Russell quickly.
"Come on, Anna."

She felt slightly irritated that Russell now seemed
to be calling the shots, butting in on what was really
her evening, but she decided to let it go. She simply
didn't have the energy or the passion to complain
about something which she was rapidly realising
meant very little to her.

The car was a limousine, at the front of which sat
a broad-shouldered driver, his face shadowed and hidden by a peaked uniform cap. Anna climbed into the
back and the first thing she spotted was a drinks cabinet. She thought it was *outrageously* over the top, and
said so.

"Don't you want a drink, then?" prompted Russell
eagerly.

Anna suppressed a shudder at the thought of intro-
ducing any more alcohol into her system. One glass
tonight had been *quite* enough! "Not unless they've
got facilities for cocoa-making!"

"Careful," warned Russell slyly, his pale eyes roving suggestively over her silver-covered body. "Too
much cocoa and we'll have the old, tubby Anna back,
instead of this gorgeous, slinky new thing!"

Anna went rigid with indignation. It wasn't so much
the fact that he had just insulted her, it was the cloy-

ingly familiar manner in which he had done so. And since when? Platonic friends did not speak to each other in that way. So did he really imagine that some photographs of her gave him the right to ogle her in that presumptuous way?

Russell slid his hand along the back of the seat as the car purred towards Knightsbridge. "You know, you're going to make a whole lot of money for me with this book of yours, baby," he slurred. "I smelt the sweet, sweet smell of success tonight!"

Anna felt slightly uneasy, but forced herself not to show it. Russell was a friend, she tried to tell herself firmly, and he was a little tipsy. No more than that. Even so, she found herself carefully edging further away from him.

"I'm very pleased to hear it," she told him briskly.

"Maybe we could make even more? The possibilities are *endless*, wouldn't you say? Huh? What do you reckon, Anna?"

"I think that I'm done with diet books and publicity," Anna answered truthfully. "It takes up too much valuable time."

"I couldn't agree more," he breathed. "Time when we could be doing infinitely more exciting things. Oh, *An-na*," he moaned.

It was like a monstrous nightmare.

Anna was aware that he had launched himself across the back of the limousine, that his arms were gripped tightly around her and that clammy, wet, alcohol-scented lips were being clamped onto her mouth with all the finesse of a lavatory plunger.

She gagged and began to pummel her fists futilely

against Russell's chest, then things began to happen very quickly.

The limo drew to a screeching halt and the chauffeur slammed his way out of the driver's seat. In a daze, Anna could see that her first impression of him as a big, strong man with immensely broad shoulders had been entirely correct, and her gratitude knew no bounds when he wrenched open the car door and leaned over the back seat where he picked Russell up by the lapels and hauled him roughly out of the car and onto a grass verge.

"You bastard!" the chauffeur ground out in the voice that Anna most wanted to hear, and she could have wept as the man lifted Russell's head up briefly, before shoving it down hard into the wet mud again.

"T-Todd," she said shakily, thinking that she must be hallucinating. "Is it really you?"

"It's really me, sweetheart," he told her, in a grim, steely voice.

And then Anna did something she had never done before in her life.

She fainted.

CHAPTER ELEVEN

ANNA opened her eyes to find herself lying on the sofa, with three anxious blonde heads hovering above her like angels.

"Mummy! Are you better?"

"Daddy says you passed out!"

"It's because you don't eat enough," scolded Tasha, who was ashen with worry.

"Bed—now!" came a stern voice from behind them as Todd walked towards her carrying a small glass of brandy, and it was a measure of how worried the girls must have been that after each gingerly kissing her cheek, they all trooped off to bed without a single objection.

Todd put the brandy down and sat on the edge of the sofa, before taking both her cold hands into the warmth of his. Anna had never seen him looking quite so pale, or so shattered. "Feeling better?" he asked her quietly.

Anna tried to smile, but her lip wobbled miserably instead. "I think so. All I can remember is a blurred car ride home." And then Todd carrying her from the car to the flat, holding onto her as if he could never bear to let her go, while she clung onto him like a loving limpet. She remembered the unfamiliar rough feel of a uniform jacket beneath her clutching fingertips. "Were you really dressed up as a chauffeur?" she questioned wonderingly.

He smiled at her dazed expression. "I really was. I brought the girls home first and got Mrs Hobbs to come over, and then I bribed the official employee to lend me his uniform." He wriggled his shoulders and allowed a smile to ease the tension he had been feeling for weeks now. "It was pretty tight across the shoulders, I can tell you!"

"What on earth made you do that?"

He gave her a steady look. "For a very good reason, as it transpires, Anna Travers! Because, despite all my attempts to reason away the suspicions I harboured about Russell's motives towards you, I was unable to get rid of my gut feeling, which was that I really shouldn't trust him."

She sipped the brandy and felt some of its warmth flood into her veins. "Wouldn't it have been simpler just to tell me?"

He stroked one palm with his thumb and sent her a rueful smile. "Much simpler, if only you would have believed me! You thought that the objections I put up about Russell were just a manifestation of my not wanting you to promote the book. Didn't you?"

"Maybe. Only your objections turned out to be well-founded, didn't they?" said Anna, closing her eyes briefly. "Oh, I wish you could have convinced me, Todd, and then none of this would ever have happened."

He shook his dark head. "Believe me, I had trouble convincing *myself* that his motives were nefarious. After all, we've known him and Saskia for years, and

I thought that their marriage was as solid as any other.''

''Me too,'' said Anna slowly. ''But then no one knows what goes on in someone else's marriage, do they?''

He shook his head and held her gaze in his. ''I came back from Romania to find you both drinking champagne,'' he told her sombrely. ''And you looked like a stranger to me—like some beautiful stranger from a magazine, not the woman I left behind. And Russell clearly thought so, too.''

''Oh, God!'' she whispered, in a hollow voice. ''Maybe he thought that I was leading him on that night! But I wasn't, Todd! I swear to you I wasn't!''

''I know that, sweetheart,'' he whispered back. ''Because of all the women I've ever met you are the only one who is completely without guile.''

''He brought the champagne round and it seemed churlish not to open it to celebrate the news about the book. And he insisted on opening another bottle, Todd—I should have stopped him. Why on earth didn't I stop him?''

Todd frowned. ''Why *should* you stop him? It isn't unreasonable to trust a man you've known for years, you know, Anna. And especially a man whose wife is a good friend of yours. I thought that I must be imagining things, going mad even, when I suspected that he desired you in the most elemental way possible.''

''And yet that night in bed, once he'd gone, you forced yourself to apologise for your suspicions,'' said Anna wonderingly.

''Because I wondered myself if my suspicions were based on fact, or simply on jealousy.''

"Jealousy?" she asked him, surprised.

"Uh-huh." He lifted one of her hands to his mouth and kissed it. "While I was away you had undergone the most secret and stunning transformation and it took a little getting used to. I wondered if the way I felt didn't have something to do with the fact that I wasn't *used* to men looking at you in that way. And I didn't like it!

"Plus *I* had just come back from spending time in Romania with Elisabeta, and, as you quite rightly said, trust isn't a one-way street. And I trusted *you*, Anna; that was never in any doubt. Once I had calmed down I realised that. It was Russell who was the problem. But I still felt that I owed you an apology."

"I should never have got into that car with him."

He pulled her into his arms. "I don't think he would have *raped* you, sweetheart."

"Where is he now?"

"Where I left him. Lying in the gutter, where he belongs."

"You don't think he'll get run over?"

He smiled in spite of himself. Even when someone had wronged her, she still had a soft heart! "I was speaking metaphorically, sweetheart. I actually left him on the grass verge."

"What the hell am I going to do about Saskia?" she groaned.

"That depends on whether Russell tells her anything. Or on whether this kind of thing has happened before. It won't be easy, because something like this irrevocably affects a friendship. Her dear husband," he added grimly, "failed to think of *that*, too."

"Oh, Todd," said Anna suddenly as she thought of

her family—the most valuable gift she had ever been given. "Let's go and look at houses in the country tomorrow."

He eyed her very carefully. "Geographical escape?" he hazarded. "To get you out of a situation which could get difficult?"

She shook her head. "No. More than that—much more. It's time for a change," she told him fervently. "Just like you said. These years are so very precious, Todd, and we can never get them back. Let's give the girls fresh air and roses in their cheeks. And let's give the three of them more time with us," she concluded softly.

"And what about your new career? The next book? And the book after that?"

Anna shook her head. "I could do that from anywhere."

"Yes, I know."

"But I don't think I want to, Todd. It's too intrusive—they want too much of *me*. And the girls have just finished that particular chapter of their lives, so it seems pretty dumb for me to open another one! We certainly don't need the money, so I'm going to give all the proceeds of *Premium Wand* to a children's charity."

His grey eyes lit up with pride. "Sure?"

"As sure as I am that I love you."

He grinned. "Oh, well. In *that* case…"

EPILOGUE

THE late afternoon sunshine warmed the grey stone of
the sprawling country house, while the drowsy hum of
bees gave the atmosphere a dream-like quality.

But life was like that these days, thought Anna happily. Sometimes she actually had to pinch herself to
remind herself that she had found her dream; they all
had—and they were living it.

She heard the chinking of delicate china as Todd
made his way from the house towards the terrace, carrying a tray of tea. He somehow managed to look so
masculine and so...so...*desirable*, thought Anna, that
it was as much as she could do not to confiscate the
tray and drag him back up to their beautiful bedroom,
which overlooked the apple orchard and was right at
the far end of the house from their rapidly growing
and ever-curious triplets!

In a minute or two, the girls would use the amazing
sense they had developed to sniff out food—especially
cake!—and would come tearing down to demolish
most of it!

Todd grew closer and Anna was able to feast her
eyes on him, unobserved. He was wearing faded blue
jeans and a white tee-shirt and his brown feet were
bare. He looked much more casual and far more relaxed than the city Todd she had grown to know and

to love, and her love for him grew with every day that passed.

For Todd had discovered that life in the slow lane could be immensely rewarding. He still retained an interest in the companies which appealed to him and money continued to roll in, despite the fact that he devoted much less time to business and much more to his family.

They had kept on the flat in Knightsbridge, with the intention of going up to London whenever they chose to. The fact that they rarely did so had proved something of a shock to Anna—but she was as contented as the rest of her family, living deep in the heart of the country.

They had intended to buy an elegant Georgian town house near the centre of Winchester where they could stable Tally's horse nearby, but they had ended up in a rural idyll at the bottom of a lane lined with cow-parsley and studded with primroses in the spring. They had been passing the house quite by chance one day, when Tina had spotted the "For Sale' notice.

And as Todd said, they didn't choose the house, the house chose *them*! And the isolation which Anna had feared had simply failed to materialise. These days she took pleasure in the simplest things, but the greatest pleasure of all was watching her daughters blossom and spending time with her husband—away from the pressures of city life.

As for her career as a dietary guru, Anna had let it die a natural death. *Premium Wand* had topped the non-fiction best-sellers' list for almost fourteen weeks, and Anna had gone ahead with her decision to donate all the profits to a children's charity, and had declined to do a follow-up. The publishers had been irritated by her decision, but Anna had shrugged her shoulders and told them, "Tough!" After all, she wasn't living her life solely to please the publishers!

The other really *big* news was that Elisabeta had married an American banker who was pouring thousands of dollars into making her family's wine the most drinkable in the country! She and Scott Adams were now the proud parents of a baby girl named Ioana, after Elisabeta's late mother, and the three of them were due to visit the Travers family that summer.

The news had come as no surprise to Todd and Anna recalled his curiously unworried attitude when he had returned to England after Elisabeta's mother's death. When the news of the engagement had come through he'd told Anna that he had met Scott at the funeral and had instinctively known that a secure relationship would follow. He had even broached the subject with Elisabeta but she had begged him not to mention it until a year had elapsed, as a mark of deference to her mother. And Todd had done as she asked, had kept completely silent on the subject, until Elisabeta had deemed that the time was right to announce her engagement.

Yet another reason to respect and love the man, thought Anna adoringly as Todd walked across the garden towards her.

Todd put the tea-tray down on the white wrought-iron table and tipped Anna's straw hat back so that he could see her face, and when he could stared down very hard at her.

She wrinkled her freckle-dusted nose. "What?"

He smiled, and shook his head while he sat down

and poured tea for them both. "I was just thinking how happy and contented you look."

"Well, I am—that's probably why," she teased, then thought of something else and frowned. "Todd..."

"Mmm?"

"Did you like me better when I was fat or when I was thin?"

"You weren't *ever* fat!" he corrected her sternly.

"Stop procrastinating and tell me!"

He looked at her assessingly. "I like you the same whatever you are."

The expression in his eyes said more than his words and she found herself blushing at the ripe old age of thirty—now that *did* make her feel young again! "Well, love, then," she amended. "Do you love me more as a skinny or a fatty?"

"Ditto!" He smiled. "I don't think of you in terms of a body shape, Anna. What draws me to you is what has always drawn me to you—your sweetness and your softness, the way you care so deeply for those around you."

"But what about...?" Her voice faltered.

He saw the confusion in her eyes and guessed its source immediately, but communication was a little like having a second language—the less you used it, the rustier you got! "But what?" he prompted, wanting *her* to say it.

"Sex," she whispered. "Is it better with a cushioned, voluptuous body, or with a sleek, streamlined one?"

"It's absolutely bloody gorgeous because it's with *you*, my darling," he told her simply, then gave a slow smile. "And if you like we could leave our tea and remind ourselves of just how gorgeous it is!"

In a minute she would let him lead her upstairs. But there was something she needed to do first...

"That sounds wonderful, Todd, but before we do there are a couple of things I want to tell you."

A watchful gleam appeared in the silver-grey eyes. "Oh?"

"You know the idea of me having a career?"

She saw the sudden immobility which froze his features.

"Yes," he said carefully.

"Remember what you said? That you wouldn't object if I discovered something I really wanted to do?"

"I remember."

"Something which *could*, in theory, take us back to London to live."

"That's right," he nodded.

"And is that still okay with you?"

There was a pause. "If that's what you want, Anna, then you have my blessing."

She knew from his voice how much that simple statement must have cost him. "Thank you for that, Todd," she said, in a low voice.

"And have you?" he queried, trying to put all the enthusiasm she deserved into his voice. "Found something?"

Oh, how she loved him! "I have."

"Not another diet book?" he asked quickly.

"No, not another diet book."

Todd breathed a silent sigh of relief. "But fulfilling, I hope?"

"Oh, *terribly* fulfilling," she agreed.

Their eyes met, the question in his answered silently by the rapture which shone from hers.

"Anna?"

She nodded. "Yes. I'm pregnant, Todd!"

He leapt to his feet and pulled her up into his arms, and he was laughing and so was she, and when the laughter stopped the kissing began and *that* was only stopped by the sound of three voices proclaiming in unison, "Oh, *yuk*!" as three healthy-looking twelve-year-olds came striding towards them.

"Can we tell them?" he whispered. "Or is it too soon?"

She shook her head. "We'll *have* to tell them, because otherwise they're bound to guess!"

He took her hand in his. "Still, at least it's only one this time." He looked at her questioningly. "At least, I'm *presuming* it's only one?"

Anna's eyes shone with love and pride. "That's the second thing I've got to tell you!"

As Tally approached, she pulled off her riding hat and frowned. "Mummy—why has Daddy gone so pale?"

And Anna squeezed Todd's hand tightly as she sat them down to tell them!

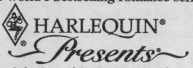

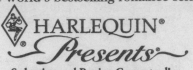

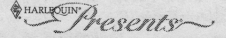

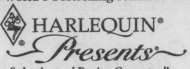